FAKE LOVE

D1453234

Fake Love

A CRAWFORD BROTHERS NOVEL

JILLIAN DODD

Jillian Dodd, Inc.
Madeira Beach, FL
Jillian Dodd is a registered trademark of Jillian Dodd, Inc.

Photo: © Regina Wamba
Cover Design: Mae I Design
Editor: Jovana Shirley, Unforeseen Editing

ISBN: 978-1-953071-19-4

BOOKS BY JILLIAN DODD

Kitty Valentine

Kitty Valentine dates a Billionaire
Kitty Valentine dates a Doctor
Kitty Valentine dates a Rockstar
Kitty Valentine dates a Fireman
Kitty Valentine dates an Actor
Kitty Valentine dates the Best Man
Kitty Valentine dates a Cowboy
Kitty Valentine dates a Hockey Player
Kitty Valentine dates Santa

Crawford Brothers

Vegas Love
Broken Love
Fake Love

Spy Girl®

The Prince
The Eagle
The Society
The Valiant
The Dauntless
The Phoenix
The Echelon

Girl off the Grid

PROLOGUE
A RECIPE FOR DISASTER.

Carter

"IT'S FREEZING OUT here," my little sister, Chloe, says as she hands me a beer. "Our brother Cade just married Palmer, the love of his life, and announced they are having a baby, yet you're out here, looking all depressed."

"Just needed some air. I'm happy for them, but I'm getting a little sick of all the mushy love stuff."

"You're lying. You're out here, thinking about Vale," she says.

And she's right. I'm thinking about how I bought Vale a ring and am considering doing something crazy—proposing to her on New Year's Eve.

"And I, for one, love the mushy love stuff. Think about it. Mom will get off our backs about having grandchildren now, thanks to Palmer."

"Do you want that for yourself?" I ask her.

"Hell no." She takes a pull of her beer. "I like meeting and sleeping with different people. It's fun.

Exciting. When I was in Paris, I met the most amazing people, including an incredible lover."

"But you didn't want—"

"More? No. At least, not right now. But you do, don't you? You've always been the marrying kind."

"You think I'm the marrying kind?" I ask, surprised.

"Yeah, I do, Carter. You, out of all my brothers, are. You're a good guy. Genuinely nice."

"*Nice*? I'm nice?"

"Nice isn't a bad thing, but Cash and Cade are both stubborn and quick to react. You've always been even-keeled. It's why you were always the best athlete in the family. Nothing flustered you. Didn't matter if you were up twenty or down twenty, you always played with the same level of intensity. You need to do that in your life, Carter, because *sex* is not the way to a girl's heart, and neither is apathy."

"Apathy?"

"Remember that time when Vale didn't show up to our family vacation?"

"Yeah, but what's that got to do with anything?"

"I overheard you talking to her on the phone afterward—all even and sweet. Fuck that. You want to be the starter? You gotta act like it. You can't be all, *Put me in if you feel like it, Coach*. Because all you are to her right now is a good lay. A booty call.

"She invited you to Fashion Week back in October. Do you know what a big deal that was for her? It was announcing to everyone in her world that she liked you. And you went. But what happened after that? Did you send flowers?"

"Uh, no."

"Did you romance her with anything *other* than your dick?"

"Um, not really."

She raises her eyebrows at me.

Fuck.

"I know you can't keep a secret to save your life, Chloe, but I'm going to tell you anyway. I bought a ring. I plan to surprise Vale at her New Year's Eve party. I'm going to propose."

"And she doesn't know you're coming?"

"I told her I wasn't sure if I could make it."

"Sounds like a recipe for disaster," she says, "but to each his own." She pats me on the back. "At least you're gonna get off the bench and do something."

CHAPTER ONE
I'M DESPERATE.

Vale

"YOU KNOW I love you, but I just can't commit to a family wedding. Sorry, baby," a deep voice says through my phone. "But we should get together soon."

I don't bother with a response, just end the call, sigh heavily, and dramatically throw the phone onto the couch next to me.

This is ridiculous. I'm a supermodel. My face is splashed across the covers of magazines. I travel around the world. Wear designer clothing. I meet new people all the time!

It shouldn't be this hard to find a damn date for my little sister's wedding.

Why I need a date so badly that I'd be willing to take a man off the street instead of going alone is complicated. My relationship with my family—my father mostly—just isn't great. You'd think after all I'd accomplished, he would be proud of me, but he isn't. It was a big disappointment when I broke up with my childhood sweetheart and left our small farm town—a place I swore I'd never set foot in again—to follow my dreams.

There are a lot of reasons why I shouldn't go home.

My dad will tell me I'm wasting my time, chasing fame, that it's fleeting.

My mother will remind me that my biological clock is ticking.

Which will lead them to remind me that I still could have the life they always wanted for me. That it's not too late. That I could settle down with said childhood sweetheart, Trent, who isn't married yet.

And it just so happens that Trent will be the best man at the wedding.

After my last-resort date fails me, I consider canceling at the last minute, pretending that I need an emergency appendectomy or something.

But the second I think it, the phone rings.

It's my sister calling.

I answer and find out she's upset.

Really upset.

And it breaks my heart, hearing her worry about the wedding. Her future. And I know that I could never miss that.

I know what I have to do.

I scroll through my phone one more time, stopping on the name of a man I should have deleted months ago but didn't have the strength. Because just seeing his name causes my heart to beat faster.

Carter Crawford.

He's the only man I've ever considered settling down with.

The only man since I left the farm to invite me to spend time with his family.

The only man who has broken my heart.

I *must* be desperate.

CHAPTER TWO
THE ANSWER IS NO.

Carter

My phone rings.

A glance at the screen tells me who is calling, and I answer the phone with a firm, "No."

"You didn't even hear what I have to say," Vale says, her voice always as silky smooth as I know her lips to be.

"Don't need to. The answer is no."

"Carter, please, I'm desperate."

"How desperate?" I ask, squinting my eyes as my dick springs to attention.

"My little sister is getting married, and I'm calling to ask you to go home with me desperate."

"Compared to being in jail, foodless, homeless, or injured, I'd say that isn't very high on the desperation chain."

"Fine. I'm literally outside your door, on my knees, begging desperate."

"On your knees desperate?" *Interesting.* I set down the smoothie I just made, walk to my front door, and

open it—surprised to find her there and actually on her knees. I can't help but smirk. "Not that long ago, I would have found this exciting. But you *do* look desperate."

"*Our flight leaves in three hours* desperate."

"Three hours? How long have you known about the wedding?"

"Early January."

"January? It's April. And you, of all people, haven't been able to find a date?"

"Carter, I can explain. And I will. I promise. But right now, I need you to go pack."

"I'm not going anywhere with you." Because I am not. I can't. Like, I'd do it for *anyone* but her.

The last time we spoke was when she called and asked how my new year was going. She had that accusatory tone in her voice. The kind women use when they say one thing but really mean another. She thought I hadn't shown up for her party and was trying to call me on it. Needless to say, I wasn't having any of that. And when she asked if we could get together the following week when she was back in town, I was still hurting from what had really happened and let her have it. Told her, no, we couldn't get together. And then I told her that on New Year's Eve, as the clock struck midnight, I realized that she was not the girl for me. I gave her the easy way out—plus, I didn't want to hear her excuses. I couldn't handle it. I was a broken mess.

We haven't spoken since.

She gets tears in her eyes. "You have no idea what it's like to be a disappointment to your family."

"You're a supermodel who travels the world," I scoff.

"Which is the opposite of what they wanted." She gets to her feet. "Please, Carter."

"Why me?"

She looks down and whispers, "Because there is no one else."

"No one else? You run out of boy toys?"

"I liked you, Carter. A lot. What you said on the phone the last time we talked really hurt."

"I'll say," I mutter. Even though it's been almost four months, I'm still not over her. I honestly don't think I'll *ever* be over her.

"I'm just saying that I understand you aren't the least bit interested in me, but if you aren't dating anyone, could you possibly find it in your heart to pretend for just one weekend that you still find me irresistible? We always had so much fun together."

I wouldn't have to pretend, I think.

"What's in it for me? I have plans this weekend," I lie.

"Fine. You want to negotiate, Carter Crawford? Let's do it."

The determined look in her eye when she wants something is one of the sexiest things about her. Sure, she's a supermodel, and she has a beautiful body, but I was always most attracted to her drive. Her passion for life. She is one of the few people who can go toe-to-toe with me in an argument and not back down.

I have to bite my lip to keep from smiling and thinking about how she could practically wrap me around her little finger. How the second she used to call and say she was in town, it would convince me to drop everything and spend time with her.

"The top-rated offensive lineman in the country, AJ Barnett, will be at the wedding. He's projected to go high in the upcoming draft. And happens to be the groom."

"Yeah, that's not much of an enticement," I say, still trying to play it cool, but when she's near me, I feel anything but. "I've already spoken to him. His family decided to go in a different direction."

"I know *for a fact* that he hasn't signed a representation contract yet."

"Are you telling me that with the draft less than two weeks away, he is agentless?" My eyes go wide.

"Yes. You'd be doing me a favor and have the chance to earn some major coin. The kid is a specimen, and I happen to know that offensive guards are some of the highest-paid players in the league because it's their job to protect the quarterback's blindside. Please, Carter," she says, folding her hands in prayer. "I need you."

The way she says she *needs me* cuts through me.

"Fine," I agree.

Her big, beautiful eyes fill with tears, and she looks up at me and says, "Thank you."

OFFICIALLY LOST IT.

Vale

CARTER TURNS HIS back on me, walking inside. And what a fine back it is. He's shirtless, wearing only a pair of sweatpants, and I can't help but sigh as I follow him.

I love Carter's house. Actually, I loved the man who lives in it.

"Where are you going?"

"Well, I just got back from my jog, so I'm going to drink the smoothie I was making when you rang the doorbell, and then I'm going to shower."

"Oh, okay, yeah," I say, my brain becoming even more frazzled over the sight of his naked chest. I used to love to lay my head on that chest and listen to his heartbeat. I used to love being wrapped in those strong, muscular arms.

"Come in my closet," he says as memories of him frantically stripping off my clothes and setting me up on his kitchen island replay in my head. "I'll pick out some clothes. You can pack them while I shower."

Each step I take through his house, I remember something else. Other details. If I were watching the movie of my life, this is where they would insert a musical montage of all the fun, flirting, drinking, passionate sex, and morning-after pancakes we always had.

His whole house holds memories for me. And it sort of stings now.

"What events are we attending? Where are we staying? How formal will it be?" Carter asks.

"Couple's shower, bachelor and bachelorette parties, picnic with games, wedding rehearsal, night-before dinner, and then golf and the wedding and reception. It will be an outdoor wedding on the family farm."

I watch as he takes out a suitcase and sorts through his clothing very quickly and efficiently. Very much the way I do. The telltale sign of someone who is often on the road.

But he's not moving fast enough.

I shove our boarding passes in front of him, which note how little time we have left. "We really have to hurry, Carter."

"I'm not flying commercial, Vale. What time do you have to be there?"

I notice he says *you*, not *we*. But he's pulling out clothing.

"Uh, the couple's shower is tonight at seven."

He gets on his phone, calls someone, and sets up a flight. Then, he points at a suitcase and walks into the bathroom, closing the door tightly behind him.

The sound of the shower running sets my mind on fire, burning with past scenes of us showering together. Of the way he looked wet, the way the water ran down his body, seemingly perfectly placed to highlight everything from his model cheekbones and strong jaw to his muscular shoulders.

I shake my head and get to packing, folding his clothing carefully to avoid wrinkles, placing them inside packing cubes, and layering them inside his suitcase.

I don't zip the bag up yet because I expect that he will have some toiletries to add.

What I don't expect is for him to walk back into his closet, wet and wrapped in nothing but a towel.

I can't help but hope—make that pray—he will drop the towel and get dressed in front of me. If he did though, I wouldn't be able to stop myself from straight-up throwing myself at him.

A good shag would do wonders to break the ice between us.

Sadly, he chooses a few articles of clothing and a watch and makes his way back into the bathroom. He doesn't close the door as tightly this time. From the mirror in his closet, I can see the reflection of the bathroom mirror and manage to get a brief but wondrous sliver of a view of his delicious backside.

He comes out fully dressed, throws a few final things into his bag, and says, "Let's go."

I grab his hand, causing him to pull back in shock, but I need to clear the air before I lose my nerve. "I'm not sure what happened between us, why you felt that way and cut off all contact, but if I did something wrong, Carter, I'm sorry. I really am."

"You're only apologizing because you need me. I'm assuming since it's mere hours before your flight, I'm not the first person you asked."

"Only because you made it very clear the last time we spoke that you didn't want to see me anymore, but since you agreed, there's one other thing I need to tell you."

He shakes his head at me in disbelief. "As if my going isn't enough?"

"I don't want to get into my family dynamics, but this weekend, we have to pretend to be more than friends. We need to be engaged."

Carter's jaw tenses, and he blinks his eyes before keeping them closed for a beat longer than usual, like I hit a nerve.

"No way," he says firmly.

"My parents have rules, Carter," I argue.

"What kind of rules?"

"Well, we can only sleep together in their house if we're engaged. It shows a level of commitment to them."

"Look, I'll be your date, for old times' sake or

whatever, but I *will not* be your fake fiancé. Hell, I didn't even get the official title of boyfriend when we were together." He sets his suitcase down and unzips it—the threat clear. "Seriously, I've seen that movie before. It never works out."

"In the movies, it does," I counter.

"Well, it won't for us," he says.

"I know."

"And I don't think I should sleep in the same room with you," he says sternly even though his eyes tell me a different story.

I can see—actually, feel—the fire in them every time he looks at me.

I let out a pathetic sigh and know I have to tell him. "All right, truth time. I'm the black sheep of the family. My dad is … you're lucky, Carter. Your family is close."

"Yours isn't?"

"Well, they all are, except for me. I left home. My parents haven't forgiven me."

He rolls his eyes. "I'm sure they are proud of you regardless. You're very successful."

"It doesn't matter. They don't view modeling as a serious career."

"It's earned you serious money."

"It's about family to them. Me having one, specifically. And I told them I was bringing my fiancé because, well"—I let out a sigh and roll my eyes— "my childhood sweetheart—my high school boyfriend, who they love—is still single and, unfortunately, the best man. If we're engaged, I won't have to deal with all that."

And I know I need to show him just how serious I am about this, so I reach into my bag, pull out a box from Cartier, and hand it to him.

He opens it, revealing a beautiful but simple solitaire. "You bought this?"

The look on his face is unreadable. I'm sure that's what makes him good at negotiating contracts for his sports clients. But when he narrows his eyes at me slightly, I can tell he's pissed about this, possibly even disgusted at the depths to which I have sunk.

Me too, buddy.

"It's on loan," I say quickly. "They dress me for red carpet events."

"Is it one they had lying around and sent to you, or did you pick it out?"

"Uh, what do you mean?" I ask, wondering what he's getting at.

"Did you pick out your dream ring to wear with your fake fiancé, or is it just a ring?"

My shoulders slump. "I asked them to give me something simple and classic."

"It doesn't look like you," Carter says, shutting the box and tossing it back to me before moving deeper into his closet.

I take a peek around the corner and see him getting into a wall safe.

When he starts to turn around, I pull my head back into place, so he doesn't know I was watching.

"I can't have you wearing that ring if you are supposed to be my fiancée," he says.

He holds a small box out in front of me.

I stand still. But then I finally understand what he wants me to do, and I hold out my palm, causing him to drop the box into my hand.

"Open it," he says.

And when I do, my breath catches.

"Carter!" I manage to gasp out. "This is the most gorgeous ring I've ever seen!"

I start to slip it on my finger, but then I glance up at him. He's studying me, a sad look on his handsome face.

"Wait. Where did you get this? What is it for? *Who* is it for? I heard you weren't dating anyone—"

"I'm not," he says brusquely, obviously irritated by my questions. "All that matters is, the ring is insured. Put it on, and let's get going. We don't want to be late."

Even though he didn't want to come with me, now, all of a sudden, he seems to be in a hurry.

But I just sit and stare at the ring.

He rolls a suitcase in front of me and taps his foot.

I put the ring on.

"A perfect fit," I say breathlessly.

NO SEX DIET.

Carter

ONCE WE'RE SETTLED into the plane and we have taken off, it's time to get serious about this.

First is to forget the breathless sound she made when she slipped the ring on her finger. How it was the same sound she used to make after we had sex, when she laid her head on my chest right before she went to sleep. The kind of sigh that sounded both surprised and content. Like she was always shocked but happy at how good we were together.

Second is to make a commitment to myself that regardless of if I have to sleep with her, sleeping is *all* that will be allowed. I'm on a no-sex diet for this trip.

Third is to remind myself that I am not doing this to help her out or to spend time with her again. I am not doing this because I think this is our second chance. I am doing this for one reason and one reason only. To sign her future brother-in-law, represent him in the draft, get him the best deal possible, and start tagging on endorsements.

She unbuckles her seat belt, but she doesn't look any more comfortable.

Might as well keep her that way.

"Okay, so we need to be on the same page," I say to her. "When did we get engaged? Where are the pictures? What did I say when I proposed?"

"I don't know," she says softly.

"It's the first thing they are going to ask, Vale. After they ask why you didn't call and tell them the good news when it happened."

"Fine," she says with a sigh, twirling a piece of hair around her finger. It's a nervous habit. One I happen to adore. "Before I came to your house, I might have thought about some of that. Let's go with, we've been dating on and off for a while—you know, like we were before—nothing serious. I've mentioned you to my sister in the past, so your name won't be a surprise."

"And?"

"And because of my traveling, you didn't think it would work."

"Oh, no freaking way. Don't you dare put that on me," I say with probably too much conviction for someone who isn't supposed to care.

"Fine. *I* didn't think it would work."

"So, then what happened? How did we overcome it?"

"Um, I got offered a role on a network show. The pilot did well, except one of the girls they'd originally cast annoyed test viewers. Now, they want me. They know it will be a hit. It means I'll be living in LA, where they're filming." She pauses. "Honestly, Carter, I don't know if I should take it or not. It would mean not modeling as much. Not traveling as much."

"It depends on what you want out of your life," I say simply even though the thought of us being in the same city together tugs at my heart and I want her to do that more than anything—for both of us.

She closes her eyes. When she opens them, they are filled with tears. "It doesn't matter what I want, Carter. The story is that when I came back to LA—"

"How long have you been here?" I ask, wondering why she never reached out.

"Uh, it's been about two months," she says quietly, one tear falling from the corner of her eye.

"And you didn't tell me?" I reply, feeling like I just got a blow to the gut.

She drops the piece of hair, and I focus on it as it slowly untwists, unraveling, like my life did that night.

"I … just … well, you told me I wasn't the girl for you."

I try not to show the hurt in my eyes, but I'm sure it's there.

"So, then," she finally says, "over the last two months, we rekindled things and had a whirlwind romance, and you asked me to marry you last weekend."

"And how did I do it?"

"I'm not sure," she says.

"You mean to tell me that you've never pictured yourself getting engaged or what it might be like?"

"If I'm being honest, yes, I have." She hesitates, brushing her hair back off her face. "Realistically, I didn't think for a second it was going to happen, but I will admit that I did imagine what it would be like if you proposed at my party. The clock striking midnight. Confetti raining down on us. You on one knee. A kiss that symbolized more than a year of being together."

I swallow hard, my insides churning, my heart racing. *She actually imagined me proposing?* And more importantly, she would have said yes.

She waves her hand through the air in front of her, quickly dismissing the thought. "Crazy, right? Anyway, last weekend, I was at a charity golf event and wine auction in Half Moon Bay. The hotel I stayed at sits up on a cliff overlooking the ocean."

"I'm familiar with that hotel," I tell her, but she barely pauses, like she's lost in the memory.

"There is a walking path around the golf course and the grounds. I went for a jog, and it was almost sunset by the time I was getting back. There's this wooden bridge. When you walk down it, it's like you're away from the world in some enchanted forest. There's water running underneath it and a small waterfall. The sunset was turning the trees a golden color. The moment felt almost magical." She closes her eyes and lets out a sad sigh. "I stopped and took a picture of it. When I saw how beautiful the photo turned out, the thought crossed my mind that it would be the perfect place for someone to propose." She grabs her phone and shows me the photo she took. The dreamy look quickly leaves her face.

"Gorgeous," I say more to her than the picture. Because she is more beautiful than I even remember.

"So, let's go with that. You took me up there for the weekend and proposed at sunset. We can even show them this photo."

"Wouldn't we have taken a selfie after we got engaged?"

"Uh, we did, but then your phone died. You hadn't backed it up in a few days, and we lost the photos."

"I would never do that. My phone is never allowed to get below fifty percent."

"Fine. I lost our engagement photos because I'm an idiot."

"Sounds fair," I say, raising my eyebrows and giving her a smirk. "And why didn't we tell them?"

"Because we wanted to do it in person, I would assume."

"Were you surprised?"

"What do you mean?"

"Were you surprised I'd asked you? Had you expected it? Had you picked out the ring? Had we picked it out together? Had I chosen it myself?" I ask.

"I don't know, okay?" she says, throwing her hands up in frustration. "Fuck, Carter, you're stressing me the fuck out, and I'm already stressed enough about this whole thing! You think it was easy for me to show up at your door after what you said to me?"

I don't answer her. I get up and walk away—just toward the galley, but still. I know I'm being a bit of a dick. I also know that I deserve to be, but at the same time, I don't like seeing her upset.

I know. *I know.* I should be mad at her. She should be mad at me.

This situation is ridiculous.

Preposterous.

Crazy.

But I've done crazy things in the name of love before.

In the fifth grade, I punched Jimmy Tipton in the mouth because he'd tried to hold my girlfriend's hand. Instead of going to get ice cream with me, she comforted the boy who was lying on the ground, bleeding.

In high school, I almost missed the state playoffs because my girlfriend was having a meltdown over her newly dyed hair.

In college, I once stood outside a girl's dorm, playing music to get her back.

I've always been passionate—about both girls and football. Since I got hurt, I turned that passion into getting the best deals for the athletes who allow me to be their agent.

Women were just a fun distraction.

Until I met Vale.

And did something crazy again.

Chloe had been right. It *was* a disaster.

And now, in retrospect, it upsets me to think that in my attempt to surprise her, I made her think I didn't care.

I also shouldn't have walked away.

Which is why I'm about to do something crazy again.

I pour us each a tequila on the rocks. The good stuff. Top-shelf añejo served with an orange slice, sprinkled with cinnamon.

As I do, I remember another moment in our relationship. Well, non-moment. I invited her on my family's yearly trip to Palmilla, but she said she didn't want to intrude on family time. When I pressed her on it, she told me she would come after her Costa Rica shoot but ended up bailing. Something about a last minute photo shoot.

I hadn't been seeing anyone else, but I didn't know if she was, even though we talked every day.

For someone who prides himself on being up-front with his clients, I realize that I was playing it way too cool with this girl.

I set a tequila down in front of her. "You look like you could use this."

"Is this the stuff you like? The stuff you always drink with your family in Palmilla?"

"You remember that?"

She nods slowly. "I remember the disappointment in your voice when I told you I wasn't coming."

"Was there really a last-minute shoot?"

She rolls her eyes up to the ceiling and holds up her hands in supposed defeat. "Going on your family trip felt like a big commitment."

"And now, here I am, engaged to you and off to meet yours," I quip.

I clink her glass, not bothering to offer a toast because I really have no idea what might come out of my mouth at this point.

"So, back to business. I had my sister go shopping with you. Conveniently asked you to stop at the jewelry store to pick up my watch." I point to the Cartier wrapped around my wrist. "And you did what girls do in a store like that—you stopped to dream. You fell in love with two rings"—I take her left hand in mine, observing the ring I designed just for her—"and I had one custom-made and surprised you with it. On the bridge. Just the two of us. As the sun started to set. I'd insisted we leave our phones in the hotel room because I didn't want any distractions. We might not have photos, but we have our beautiful memories of that moment."

She takes a drink of tequila, closes her eyes, leans back, and says with a sigh, "Thank you, Carter."

A few moments later, she's asleep.

With her head on my shoulder.

A LITTLE BRIDAL
FREAK OUT.

Vale

I GOT A little reprieve on the flight, but as we drive the hour from the airport to my family's farm, I get more questions from Carter, most of them about the wedding.

I finally just start flashing him my sister's Pinterest board, full of wedding details. I figure it might bore him to death, but I should know better. Carter is a details guy.

"Why are you going home again if you're so miserable?" he asks.

"Because I love my sister. And I'm the maid of honor. I haven't been around as much as I should have been, and she's always looked up to me. When she called to tell me she got engaged, she told me she was happy, but was worried she'd end up like our sisters. I handled that conversation well. I've been trying since then to find a date to the wedding. I'll be honest, I basically called every guy I knew. They all said no. And because of it, although I know it's terrible of me, I actually considered not showing up—to cancel on my baby sister at the last minute."

"What changed your mind?"

"She called me again late last night, really upset.

It wasn't a little bridal freak-out. This was about her future. Well, really, about AJ's future. His father is basically forcing him to not take on an agent. He says it's ridiculous to pay an agent when his uncle is an attorney who can look over any contract he needs and will only charge him his standard hourly rate. I need you to take care of AJ somehow so that my little sister is taken care of. If that all even makes sense."

He reaches out and softly squeezes my hand. It's hard for me not to react to his comforting gesture.

"So, you're not just in this for yourself?"

"Not entirely. And it's the real reason we need to pretend to be engaged. If we are, it would make you family too. My parents want my sister to come home. They think AJ playing professional football is a pipe dream. That *he will get hurt and won't be able to support her* kind of thing. I think it's more that they want her back home.

"Sounds crazy, but it was a big deal that she even went to college. It took guts for her to stand up to my parents. It's like they are stuck in a '50s time warp as far as a woman's role is concerned.

"I'm proud of all my sisters, but she and I are the most alike. She's beautiful too, Carter. Way prettier than I am. And smart. So smart. She's graduating with honors in May. AJ graduated in December. They wanted to get married now, so after her graduation they would be able to focus on getting settled wherever he ends up getting drafted."

"You know, you could have just told me that. I would have agreed to this crazy scheme a lot faster."

"Yeah, I know," I say with a grim smile. "But I needed to know where we stood first."

CHAPTER THREE
NO PRESSURE.

Vale

"HOLD ON A minute." Carter looks at me before looking out the car window again. "Did I just see your family's name on that bank?"

I want to slump down in my seat and cover my eyes. "Yes, you did."

"Is that *your* family? The Martins? A pretty common name after all."

"Nope. It refers to my family."

"Your family owns the bank?"

His jaw is almost on the floor at this point, and I have to wonder why. It isn't like his family hasn't done well for themselves.

"Yes, they do."

"They. Not we?"

"I don't consider myself part of it."

"Wait. The feed store has your name on it too." He glances back over his shoulder as we pass.

"Yes. And the car dealership, the farm equipment dealership, the grocery store …"

"You led me to believe you were from a farming family."

"I am. Only my father didn't want to stop at farming."

"Evidently. I need to change my expectations." He glances my way. "Anything else I need to know?"

"Other than the fact that my family owns half the town and they expected me to stick around and help work at one of their many businesses?"

"I've got you. You have nothing to worry about."

And for a second, I can almost believe him. Carter can make anything happen. He's magic.

I mean, he managed to make me consider settling down, which was something I'd never expected. It was always what I'd thought I didn't want.

So, maybe he can get me through this long weekend.

Yet as soon as we cross through town and I start noticing little landmarks signaling the last few miles before reaching the farm, I start tapping my foot nervously.

He notices. "You okay?"

"I've walked runways all over the world. I've walked red carpets. I've visited places I never dreamed I'd step foot in." I laugh a little at myself. "Why am I so freaked out about coming home?"

"It's been a long time. It's only natural."

I point down a dirt road jutting off to the right. "That leads to the fishing hole. I had a lot of fun down there as a kid. We all did."

"You fished?"

I laugh. "There are other things to do at a fishing hole besides fish. It was where we'd hang out at night. Party. Drink. That kind of thing."

"You'll have to show it to me while we're here," he says, and it kills me. There's a flirty tone in his voice. One my whole body reacts to.

We were always good together—no, better than good. The best sex I'd ever had—no doubt about it. When you threw the feelings I had for him into the mix, it elevated things even more.

Now, I have to somehow put that behind me while still pretending we're deeply, madly in love. But it's fake love.

He told me himself—I'm not the girl for him.

I clear my throat, pointing farther down the road. "My brother, Blake, once broke his leg after jumping out of that hayloft."

"He's the troublemaker, right? I remember you telling me a story about him once. Compared him to my youngest brother, Cash."

"He was as a kid, for sure. And he probably hasn't changed his ways much. But to my dad? He's the golden child. The only boy. If he wasn't so charming and lovable, I might hate him. But it's impossible."

"What about the rest of the family?" Carter asks.

"There's my oldest sister, Brooke. She's married

to Jake, who runs the car dealership, and they have four-year-old Sophie, who is the flower girl in the wedding. Second is Raine. She's married to Seth. He oversees the farming, and they have twin babies, Skylar and Sebastian, who are just over a year old. Then, there's me, Blake, and the bride, Lakelyn."

"Big family."

"Not as big as my parents would like. Prepare yourself to be asked how many kids we want and when we'll start having them."

"And what will we say to that?"

"Hmm. I suppose just that we've decided to wait a little while. Enjoy being together." I look at him. "Is that okay?"

"Why not?" he says. "It's not real anyway."

I take in a calming breath and know I'm going to need to keep reminding myself of that all weekend. There's no time to worry about it though since the car's rounding the last bend in the road. The sight of the house kicks off a stinging sensation behind my eyes, like I'm about to cry.

"Here we are," I whisper.

GONNA GO WILD.

Carter

IT'S SAFE TO say that Vale's childhood home is nothing like I envisioned.

There is a fenced-off plot of land that stretches as far as the eye can see. The house does have the country charm I was expecting with a wraparound porch, but its architecture is more Southern plantation than Midwest farmhouse.

There are towering maple trees lining the drive and one with a tire swing in the front lawn.

Off to the right is a beautiful red barn, which seems to be the center of activity.

"The couple's shower is taking place in the barn," Vale explains. Her voice has a faint, faraway quality to it, like she's saying one thing but deep in thought over something else.

"Are you okay, Vale?" I ask her, noticing how pale she looks.

She draws a deep breath, and I notice that her hands are trembling in her lap. I cover them with one of mine as I park the car behind a number of others.

"It's a lot," she admits in a soft voice. "I haven't been here in so long. What am I supposed to do? How am I supposed to act?"

She looks at me, tears filling her beautiful eyes.

She's worlds away from the confident, sophisticated, sexy woman I know. I wish I didn't want so badly to make her hurt go away. I wish every protective instinct didn't roar to life inside me. But it does.

"You're doing this for your sister," I murmur, holding her hands tight. "You're going to get through this because you love her. I'm not emotionally involved with your family, so right now, you have my permission to blame it all on me. Anything you need, I can take it. And I'll be right beside you."

"Thanks," she says, pressing her lips against my cheek. "You're one of the good ones, Carter. I really appreciate you doing this for me."

"You can get through this," I mutter softly, but as we get out of the car, I have to wonder if I'll be able to get through all this. It's going to be way too easy for me to pretend like I'm in love with this girl.

Moments later, we're surrounded by people.

"They're here!" A younger brunette with blonde highlights throws her arms around Vale. "Thank you for coming," she squeals, squeezing tight.

I'm guessing she's the bride-to-be.

Two more brunettes follow close behind. They have to be her two older sisters. They definitely share a family resemblance.

Meanwhile, a bunch of guys are already shaking my hand, asking if we need help with the bags and whether we had any trouble getting in. I can hardly answer one before another asks a question.

"Whew!" A young man with the same good looks as the rest of the family whistles at the rental car we got at the airport—a Range Rover SUV. "Nice car."

Vale gives the guy a hug and says to me, "This is my brother, Blake."

Then, she introduces me to her sisters and brothers-in-law. Meanwhile, a little girl—who I assume is Sophie—runs circles around us, jumping up and down and shouting with excitement.

I should be used to this. My family is the same way.

But I have to pretend to be something I'm not—Vale's fiancé.

Why did I agree to this again?

Oh yeah, because she was on her knees on my front porch. Because she looked so good. So sincere. And because I still love her even though she broke my heart.

"Sis, you're looking good." Blake slings an arm around her shoulders and steers her toward the barn, waving me on along with them. "BTO is gonna go wild when he sees you."

"BTO?" I ask.

"Oh, sorry," Blake says. "BTO is Big Trent Orlitz. High school friend of all of ours. Been calling him that for so long that, sometimes, I forget he has a real name."

Trent. Is that the ex-boyfriend?

I can't seem to help the jealousy I feel for any

other man, going wild when he sees Vale.

But she isn't mine. Not really.

At least, not yet.

I just have to keep my eye on the goal. And in this case, the goal isn't what she thinks it is—signing AJ. The goal is getting through this weekend without my heart getting in the way. But I still want her. And I know that I probably owe her the truth.

CHAPTER FOUR
WE'RE ENGAGED. YAY!

Vale

"VALE." MY MOM just about smothers me the second I'm close enough.

I hate to admit it, but it feels good. I didn't know until now just how much I'd missed being hugged by my mother. And I have to fight back the tears.

She's hardly aged a day—or so it seems. There are a few more crinkles around the eyes, a little bit of gray at the temples, but otherwise, she's the same sweet-faced, smiling mother I left behind when I decided to get the hell out of this town.

"Hi, Mom," I manage in spite of the tightness in my throat.

"Look at you." Her face is glowing as she holds me at arm's length, looking me up and down. "You're more beautiful than I remembered. You've been eating and taking care of yourself?"

"Of course, I have." I roll my eyes.

"Mom, come on." Lakelyn hugs me from behind. I think she was really worried I wouldn't show up.

She has no idea how close I came to backing out. "She just got here. You can't hog her."

My adorable four-year-old niece, Sophie, hops up and down next to me, curls bouncing. "I'm gonna be the flower girl!"

"I heard, sweetie! I can't wait to see your dress!"

"It's bea-u-ti-ful," she says happily. But then she looks at me. "You're my auntie, but Mama says you never come home. Is it because you don't like us?"

I bend down next to her, my eyes filling with tears, knowing all that I've missed out on because of my father. "I love you. I'm just, um, really busy with my job."

"Okay," she says, smiling at me and apparently letting me off the hook. "You're pretty. And I'm pretty too," she says, twirling around and making the skirt of the dress she's wearing fly around her. She looks at me and orders, "Spin."

"Uh …"

"You don't have to spin," Lakelyn says, "but you'd better have remembered your dress."

"I'm nothing if not an efficient packer," I tell her as Sophie gets bored with our conversation and skips away. "And as maid of honor, my job is to take care of you."

"Get ready to be put to work then. We have so much to get done." Mom's voice takes on the no-nonsense tone I remember. She always gets this way when she's busy and in charge. "The food for the shower is still up in the kitchen. Drinks too. They need to be brought down. Your sisters are decorating and might need a hand. I think we'll need more chairs too …"

"Mom, you're making me dizzy." I laugh. "Besides, there's someone I'd like you to meet before I dive in."

Carter's standing just to my left.

I reach out a hand and draw him closer. "This is Carter Crawford. Carter, this is my mother, Sarah."

She touches a hand to her chest while looking him up and down. "Oh my goodness, you're very handsome."

"Mom!" I laugh.

Carter takes it well. "Thank you, Mrs. Martin. It's lovely to meet you. I can certainly see where Vale's good looks come from."

Her checks flush. "I like him." She laughs, looking at me.

"I knew you would." I lean against him, letting my head touch his shoulder. It comes natural before I realize I'm supposed to be pretending. Honestly, it won't be much of a stretch to pretend to love Carter.

"It is so good to have you here," she gushes, touching his arm. "Please make yourself at home."

"Vale!"

I have no time to respond or to even know who shouted my name before I'm swept up in a pair of thick, muscular arms and twirled around in a circle.

"Damn, girl, you look good enough to eat! Traveling the world seems to have treated you well!"

Not until I'm on my feet, but still in his arms do I recognize Trent Orlitz. "Small-town life has treated you well too." I laugh, a little breathless.

He's looking pretty darn good himself. He's as tall and broad-shouldered and handsome as ever, but he's filled out even more and looks less like the boy I left and more like a man.

But he doesn't make my heart flip the way Carter does.

He pushes a lock of black hair away from his forehead, looking me up and down in a very obvious way. "I've been looking forward to seeing you again. I almost couldn't believe it when I heard you were Lakelyn's maid of honor."

"Well, wonders never cease," I manage with a faint laugh. Faint because I can just about feel Carter boring holes into Trent—and into me by virtue of the fact that we're standing so close together.

I take a step back, reaching for Carter. "Trent, this is Carter Crawford, my—"

"What is that?" Lakelyn squawks, grabbing my left hand and holding it close to her face.

"Vale!" my mother gasps. "Is that what I think it is? Are you two—"

"We're engaged. Yay!" I announce. Not the way I expected to announce it, but nothing ever goes quite right when it comes to my family, so I really shouldn't be surprised.

"You're getting married?" Mom just about faints on the spot while Lakelyn squeals and calls my sisters over to take a look.

Trent looks slightly stricken, but Blake claps Carter on the back and offers him a celebratory beer.

For a moment, I can almost get caught up in it. The excitement, the thrill of it, hugging, and answering questions.

Until …

"What's this? You got engaged and didn't tell your family?"

Boom. Moment over.

I turn slowly, knowing what I'll find.

The same tall, burly, imposing man whose eyes are still as sharp and intimidating as ever.

"Hi, Dad," I murmur. "I'm home."

IF YOU SAY SO.

Carter

IT DOESN'T TAKE long for me to understand why Vale was so hesitant to come home.

At first, I wondered if she was letting some past drama influence the present, but that was before I met her father.

Mr. Martin is a big man, the sort of man who takes up all the space in a room just by virtue of the fact that he's in it. The barn doesn't feel big enough for both of us as he marches our way.

Instead of acknowledging his daughter, he comes straight at me. "You intend to marry my daughter?"

"Yes, sir," I lie. Part of me wants to tell the truth, if only to avoid being shot. Not that he's carrying a gun, but I wouldn't put it past him to grab the nearest rifle.

"Dad, this is my fiancé, Carter Crawford." Vale wraps both her hands around my bicep.

Her father hasn't taken his eyes off me. "What do you do, Carter Crawford?" he asks.

"I'm a sports agent, sir. I work for—"

"A sports agent?" he sneers. "As in you're one of those guys who takes part of a man's hard-earned money all because you sat there while he signed his name on the dotted line?"

"Dad." Vale's voice has an edge to it now. "Don't do that."

"With all due respect, sir, there's a lot more to it than that," I say.

All this gets me is a snort. "If you say so. In your line of work, do they teach you it's appropriate to ask a girl for her hand in marriage without first asking for her father's permission?"

He doesn't wait for an answer before placing an

arm around my shoulders and leading me away from the barn. "Let's have a chat, Carter Crawford."

"Dad, we just got here!" Vale trots along beside us, throwing me huge, apologetic eyes.

"He can spare a minute for me, all things considered," her father counters.

There's not so much as a hint of invitation. I'm not being invited to chat with him. I'm being ordered to.

And I can play along. I'm a good negotiator. I'm good in a room. I'm used to men thinking they are smarter than me because I was an athlete myself.

Mr. Martin leads me into his house, which I see is both cozy and extremely well-appointed, steering me toward what I assume is his study and depositing me inside.

Closing the door, he looks me up and down. "So, you plan to marry my Vale."

"I do, sir. As for not asking for your blessing, it was spontaneous. My proposing, I mean. I didn't plan on asking her before speaking with you, but I guess I got swept up in the moment."

His brow furrows. "You get swept up in the moment a lot?"

"Only when your daughter is involved."

I get the feeling he wants to approve of this comment, but something holds him back.

"Your family? Tell me about them."

I happily give him the rundown. I'm incredibly

proud of my family. "I'm sort of the middle child. My older brother, Cade, is recently married, and he and Palmer Montlake are expecting their first child soon. My younger siblings are twins. Cash is married to Ashlyn Roberts." I decide to leave out the part about how they met at a wedding and drunkenly got married in Vegas that same night. "And then there's Chloe. She's a jewelry designer. My parents are still married and in love. We're very close. Take vacations together every year without fail."

"Glad to hear that. Family is everything. Legacy. Leaving something behind." He gestures to a row of framed photos on one wall.

"You have a beautiful family, Mr. Martin." Now that it seems like he might let me live, I can breathe a little easier. "And from what I noticed on the drive through town, you've built quite a legacy to pass down."

"We know how to do business in these small towns just as well as you do out in Los Angeles," he informs me with a wry smile. "It's a shame this wasn't good enough for all my children though. I have to wonder what sort of legacy a sports agent could leave for his children," he says.

"I'd like to imagine my children, should I be fortunate enough to have them, would carry a legacy of unconditional love with them, first and foremost. I am lucky enough to know what it means to be fully and truly supported in every aspect of my life by my parents. And I hope that I can do them justice by passing that on to my children. My parents taught us to work hard, be decent and fair, and to follow our hearts. Considering how well we've all done for ourselves, I think they did a pretty good job. If you're concerned about financial matters, I can assure you, there's nothing to worry about."

"Yeah, I noticed that flashy car you drove up in and the boulder on Vale's hand." He smirks. "I suppose they do those highfalutin sort of things out where you're from."

"It's been known to happen, sir."

I can tell he wants to see how easily ruffled I am. When he doesn't get anything more from me, the smirk turns to a grin.

"Make yourself comfortable for a moment while I get us something to drink."

I settle into a leather wing chair while he pours scotch for the two of us. A little early in the day for a drink maybe, but it's already been a long one. To think, I woke up this morning in my house, and it was just another Thursday.

Now, I'm accepting a drink from my supposed soon-to-be father-in-law and looking around his study. While doing so, I notice a book stacked with others on a small table behind his desk. The spine reads *VALE* in block letters.

"What's that?" I ask, accepting my drink. "A book about Vale? Embarrassing baby pictures?"

He's gruff when he responds, "A collection of Vale's work. Modeling, you know. Her photos."

I think I understand the man better than he wants me to.

"Hey, Dad?" Blake opens the door a crack and sticks his head in. "Sorry to interrupt, but we could use another set of hands out here, and AJ went to pick up chairs from the Pattersons. Could we borrow Carter?"

"Of course," Mr. Martin says.

I finish my drink and thank him before heading out to the hall with Blake.

Blake snickers, elbowing me with a gleam in his eye. "You're welcome."

CHAPTER FIVE
CATCH YOU ANY DAY.

Vale

"COME ON! WE can use all the help we can get. Unless you would like to get changed first?" Lakelyn looks at my outfit, including the heels.

I realize I should've dressed more appropriately. This is the farm, not brunch in LA.

"I've run around the barn barefoot before," I remind her. With one more look at the house, where Carter just disappeared with my father, I let her lead me back to the barn.

"I can't believe you are here *and engaged* to Carter Crawford. Why didn't you tell me that last night when I called you, crying about AJ and the draft?"

"I wanted to surprise you all with the engagement."

"You still could have told me you knew him. He represents Danny Diamond, and he's the GOAT."

"Goat?" I ask.

"Greatest Of All Time," she says with a grin.

"Why didn't you tell me that's who you've been seeing? Who you got engaged to?" She grabs my arm again and looks at the ring on my finger.

Because I didn't think he would actually come.

"I hope it's not awkward, him being here. Just because he's going to be family doesn't mean you or AJ have to discuss business with Carter. He won't even bring it up."

"I wish he would bring it up," she says with a frown.

"Carter did tell me that he reached out to AJ at some point but was told he had representation."

"Yeah, his uncle. Which is a huge mistake, if you ask me. He needs a good, experienced agent in his corner. It worries me to think of what might happen if he gets steered in the wrong direction."

"Do you think that will happen?"

She's always had a good head on her shoulders. AJ is lucky to have her.

She shrugs. "I hope not. But I doubt he'll get as good of a deal without a skilled agent telling him what to look out for. I respect whatever decision he comes to, but it affects me too. It's our future."

I take a look at her. She's so grown-up now, so smart and wise. Her dress is bright and cheerful, flowing around her thighs with each step she takes. Her hair is fashioned into a long braid.

"When did you get so grown-up?" I ask before we enter the barn.

"Oh, it happened gradually." She winks before handing me a mimosa from a table set up near the doors. "Drink up, sis. It's going to be a long weekend."

No kidding. Especially because I am probably going to have to sleep in the same room as Carter and try to keep my hands—and the numerous other body parts he knows how to make feel good—to myself.

"I can't help but feel bad for Carter," I confess to Brooke and Raine as we hang crepe paper in Lakelyn's wedding colors of pink and cream. "I can only imagine what Daddy's saying to him up there."

"I was afraid Seth might wet his pants when he got the big talk," Raine whispers, giggling. "And he had known Daddy for years."

"Your guy is a big-shot agent though," Brooke reminds me. "I'm sure he's probably used to intense negotiations."

"Neither of you are helping."

But I can't help laughing a little. It's like no time has passed at all. We've fallen right back into our roles. Maybe that's what being siblings is all about.

"You have to tell us all about how he popped the question!" Mom says, interrupting us. She is beside herself with excitement.

"This weekend is all about Lakelyn," I insist, eyeing the bride-to-be.

I also can't help but take note of Trent standing

on the other side of the barn, taking a sudden interest in what I have to say.

"I want to hear it!" Lakelyn claps her hands, bouncing on the balls of her feet.

I'm standing on a ladder, which doesn't help since I'm now the center of attention. "So, uh, we were at a charity golf event at a hotel on a cliff overlooking the ocean."

"Ooh," Brooke sighs.

She's already swept away, and I haven't gotten into the story yet.

"We went out to watch the sunset. And I should've probably known something was up when he suggested we leave our phones in the room, so we wouldn't have any distractions."

I have total command of the room now. If a pin dropped, we'd hear it.

"He took me down a walking path that goes around the property and had views of the ocean …" I pause for a second. "And there were rose petals leading up to a wooden bridge."

Note to self: make sure to tell him about the rose petals.

"And there were lanterns floating on the water under the bridge."

And about the lanterns.

"It was magical." I sigh, knowing I'm getting way too caught up in this fantasy. But I can't seem to stop myself. "And as the sun was about to set, it was all low in the sky, and it gave the trees surrounding us this golden glow. It was like being in an enchanted forest. Just the two of us."

"I can hardly breathe," Raine whispers while my mother fans herself.

"And a string quartet was playing on the other side of the bridge." *Because why not?* "And as they played, Carter dropped to one knee and …" I can't bear to say the actual words, the words I wish he would say to me for real. "Well, I don't want to tell you exactly what he said. Um, because it's personal."

I have to turn my face away a little because I almost convinced myself it'd all actually happened. I can practically see it in front of me—and the weight of the ring on my finger isn't helping me keep my fantasy separate from reality.

"I'm crying. I can't believe it." My mother laughs, wiping a hand under her eyes.

I am such a terrible person for lying like this.

"Anyway, that's how it happened." I shrug with a way-too-sunny smile.

Which is when Sophie runs into the ladder I'm standing on and it tips to the side. The next thing I know, I'm falling.

And then landing in a pair of strong, familiar arms.

"Hey there." Trent laughs, holding on to me. "We can't have the maid of honor breaking an arm right before the wedding."

"Thank you," I can hardly breathe. My heart's racing so fast. And it's not because I am this close to Trent again. I'm still wrapped up in my engagement fantasy.

Trent pulls me in a little closer. "I'd catch you any day, Vale."

"Hey!" Blake strolls into the barn with Carter beside him. "I freed your boy, sis!"

Carter's expression changes from amusement to anything but when he sees me in Trent's arms, and for a moment, he actually looks jealous.

But he isn't, and he never will be, and I need to remember that.

SO ROMANTIC.

Carter

I'M NOT SURE how I feel about this.

No. Wait. I am sure.

I hate it.

This Trent—*BTO*—guy makes a big show of putting Vale down on her feet. "There you go. Safe and sound," he says, yet he still holds her by the waist, and it's a little too close for my comfort.

For the first time since we started this charade,

I'm glad we're supposed to be engaged. It gives me a legitimate reason to do what I'm about to do.

I take a few long strides toward her and possessively wrap my arm around her, pulling her close to me. "Can't leave you alone for a second, can I?"

Fortunately, she places her arms around my neck. "No, you can't, and you shouldn't," she says sexily.

But I see right through it. Both of us are not-so-subtly letting old Trent know he needs to back the fuck off, just for different reasons.

He doesn't seem to get the hint though. He kisses the back of her hand and says, "I'll always be here to rescue you." Then, he tips his hat at her and goes back to whatever the hell he was doing before.

"I guess I missed out on all the excitement."

Her smile goes wide. "You did actually. Before I fell off the ladder, I was telling everyone about the proposal."

"Oh, Carter," Mrs. Martin says, her hands folded and a smile on her face. "I love how there were rose petals and lanterns and the string quartet. So incredibly romantic."

Of course, I'm thrilled she's happy about whatever Vale told her, but none of that was in our prepared proposal story.

"It was all so romantic and spontaneous," Vale gushes toward her mom as she grabs my hand, squeezing it tightly, letting me know to just roll with it.

"Romantic, yes. Spontaneous, no. I knew I wanted to marry you the first time I met you," slides out of my mouth. It's the God's honest truth but not something I ever dared to tell her.

She looks at me, her head tilted in question. "Really?"

"Hey! Look who's back!" Lakelyn says, causing Vale to turn her attention toward the barn's entrance.

Lakelyn runs out of the barn and launches herself at her six-foot-five, three-hundred-pound fiancé, AJ Barnett.

"I hope this will be enough chairs, Mrs. Martin." AJ gestures to the bed of his pickup truck. "I couldn't fit any more."

"That should be perfect, sweetheart. Thank you." Vale's mother strikes me as the polar opposite of her husband. She's sweet, soft, and kind, and she has the sort of friendly, open smile that puts you at ease.

Vale takes my hand and leads me over to AJ— I'm sure to introduce us.

Just as she starts to open her mouth, AJ turns toward us, looks at me, and says, "You're Carter Crawford, aren't you?"

"Guilty." I shake his hand.

"Carter is Vale's fiancé!" Lakelyn says. "Isn't that cool?"

"It is," he says, but the smile doesn't quite reach his dark eyes, and he quickly turns and starts unloading his truck.

And I guess I can't blame him. I know what a guy like him goes through before the draft. I was going through it myself before I got hurt.

Vale pulls me aside as everyone else starts focusing on getting the chairs set up. "AJ acted a little cold toward you. Sorry."

"I'm sure he's just surprised that you are engaged. Like everyone else has been."

"And I'm sorry about embellishing all the proposal stuff," she whispers into my ear. I have to ignore the way her breath tickles my skin.

"So long as you made me look good."

She giggles, leaning against me. When I stiffen, her eyes meet mine. "What?"

"Nothing. Just …" I glance around. We're generally being ignored in favor of last-minute shower prep. "This is hard. Your family is nice. I feel bad, lying to them. And it's hell, being this close to you."

She stiffens before standing up straight and bolting backward. "Well, I'm sorry that I'm so unattractive."

"I didn't mean that—"

"Whatever. You agreed to this, and that means you have to at least pretend."

"I know that—"

"But, hey, if it bothers you too much, I guess I could go hang out with Trent instead."

I can feel my blood starting to boil over as Mrs.

Martin calls out to us, "I nearly forgot my manners. We dragged you into setting up before you even had a chance to get settled. Vale, you'll be staying in your old room. It's all ready and waiting for you both."

"You're going to let us share a room?" she asks.

Her mom laughs, waving a hand. "Well, you are engaged after all."

DROWNING IN LUST.

"*THIS* IS OUR bed?"

"Yes," I tell him.

"It looks small."

"What, are you afraid we might brush against each other in our sleep?"

He just sighs and starts unpacking.

I should let it go, but he pissed me off in the barn. And I can't. "What's the big deal? It's not like we've never shared a bed."

He mutters something with his back turned.

"What was that?"

"Nothing."

"It sounded like you said something about Trent."

His shoulders rise and fall when he sighs. "I said, maybe you should share a bed with good old *BTO* since he's obviously still lusting after you."

"Please. That was over years ago."

Is he jealous? I don't want to let myself believe it, but what other reason would there be for him to act this way?

"I don't think it's so *over* for him."

"Please."

"Whatever," he says, taking his clothes out of his suitcase and hanging them in the closet. "It's obvious he still has a thing for you."

"Well, unfortunately for Trent, we are engaged. And I'm crazy about you."

"You didn't look too crazy about me when you were in his arms."

"Are you jealous?"

"No, actually, I am not," he says. "But you wanted this whole charade. The least you could do is show some respect for our fake relationship and not flirt with him in front of me."

"How am I supposed to do that?" I say, moving toward him and invading his personal space. We're so close that I can practically feel his chest rise and fall. "When my being this close to you is hell?"

He shakes his head at me. "It's not really a conversation we needed to have in front of your family. But now that you've brought it back up and we are alone, it *is* hell, being this close to you." He slides his hands up my back. "Because we were good together."

"*Were*," I emphasize the past tense at the same time I feel my body heating up.

"And not being able to have you puts me in hell."

"Who says you can't have me?" I blurt out. Because right now, that's all I want. Us tangled up in the sheets of my little bed. Naked. For days.

That's how it was whenever I was with him. Sure, we'd go out for dinner with friends sometimes. But for the most part, our time was spent alone. Usually in bed. *Or somewhere.* Having the most amazing, sensual sex.

I close my eyes and can practically feel his lips gliding across my neck.

"*I say* I can't have you," he answers, pulling back.

"I'm still not over you," I tell him.

"And I think you're just saying that because you need me to be your fake fiancé. I think we need to set a few ground rules. When we're with your family, we will flirt and act like we are in love, but the second we cross this threshold, we go back to what we are in real life."

"And what's that?" I ask.

"Nothing," he says.

And that breaks my heart. Again.

He doesn't say anything else, just strips his shirt off and tosses it onto the bed.

I have to look away from the chest I love. The washboard stomach I know so well. How many times did I allow my tongue to dance across those abs? And then there are his shoulders. The ones I clung to, dragged my nails over—

"I think we should both get a little more casual, don't you?" He drops his pants next.

I don't know what to do anymore. My skin's on fire along with a sudden warmth in certain other parts of my body.

"So, what? We strip for each other? That's your idea of casual?"

"I meant for the shower."

"You want to take a shower with me? Now? But I thought—"

An amused look forms on his face. "I was referring to the couple's shower. Tonight."

CHAPTER SIX
ARTS AND CRAFTS.

Carter

VALE SEEMS TO have no idea what she does to me every time she touches me.

The way her hand casually brushes against mine.

The swell of her breast against my arm when she leans in to murmur in my ear.

I understand why we have to look close. In my brain, I know it.

The rest of me is another story. She has no idea how I'm struggling against the flood of memories when her body presses against mine.

We are sitting in a circle with all the other guests. Lakelyn and AJ are in the middle, opening shower gifts.

"I love it!" Lakelyn squeals, holding up a blender. "Thank you so much!"

"What are you doing?" I ask Vale, noticing how she writes something down in a notebook every time her sister unwraps a gift.

"I have to keep track of who gave what," she

explains, "so she can write thank-you cards. It's the maid of honor's duty."

"What other duties do you have?" I can't help but wonder.

"Your guess is as good as mine," she confesses out of the corner of her mouth. "I'm only doing what I'm told."

Meanwhile, Brooke and Raine are taping the many ribbons and bows from each gift onto a paper plate.

There's a reason men don't usually come to these things.

AJ seems to be taking it all in stride. He wears a goofy grin, which I can only attribute to being deeply in love with his girl. He's happy to see her happy.

I just wish watching it didn't make me imagine myself in his shoes. About to marry the girl of my dreams.

Now, all that's left of those fantasies are bruised pride and the ring now shining on Vale's hand.

"Oh, it's a pasta maker!" Lakelyn is beside herself. She seems like a genuinely good person, truly thrilled with each gift. "Thank you so much for getting this, Aunt Helen!"

"Dinner at Lakelyn's!" Blake grins from his side of the room, where most of the men are gathered.

I decide to take a stroll over there and get away from the estrogen for a while.

Blake immediately hands me a beer. "This'll be

you soon enough." He winks. "Looking forward to it?"

"Oh, it's always been my dream to have bits of glitter all over me for days after unwrapping gifts," I say as AJ brushes more glitter from his pants.

Blake laughs. "Then, you'll have a great time with us tonight. From what BTO and I have planned, we'll all be covered in glitter by the time the night's over, if you catch my drift."

I have a sneaking suspicion I know what he's talking about but decide to play innocent. "Arts and crafts?"

"Strip club, my man. We have a stretch limo all set to pick us up at nine. It's an hour drive. We pregame in the limo and then settle in for the real party once we arrive."

"Sounds like fun." Really, it sounds like the most boring, generic bachelor party imaginable, but we're in the middle of Iowa. I guess there are only so many options.

"You're in then? Come on," he insists when I pull a face. "You've got to come. Consider it your initiation into the family."

How am I supposed to say no to that?

"I'll have to check with Vale first, make sure she's okay with it."

"She got you wrapped around her finger, huh? Like she's never raised a little hell of her own." He snorts.

I make a mental note to ask later just what sort of hell she raised.

"What else is planned for this weekend?" I ask, taking a sip from the longneck bottle in my hand while keeping an eye on Vale. I can't help it. She's a beacon, constantly drawing me in.

When she showed up at my door this morning, she looked gorgeous as always, but now that she's changed into jeans and pulled her hair into a messy braid, she looks wholesome. The smoking-hot farm girl who lives next door. And I like it. *A lot.*

"Tonight's the bachelor party, and then tomorrow, we're doing all kinds of games and such."

"Games?"

He waves a hand. "Mom's idea. We did it for Brooke and Raine, too, when they got married. You know, hay-baling. Cornhole. Football."

"The women play football?"

"Nah, they cheer us on. This is men stuff. The girls throw a big picnic together and make sure there's enough cold drinks." Blake looks me up and down. "You think you could handle a game of football?"

"I think I can manage."

If he doesn't know about my college career, that's fine. Let him think I'm some California surfer boy who has never held a football.

This might actually end up being fun.

"We'll have the rehearsal tomorrow evening,

followed by the best barbecue you'll ever have in your life. Saturday's the wedding, and then Sunday, we'll have a big breakfast and wish we hadn't drunk so much the night before."

"Some traditions don't change, no matter where you happen to live," I muse while Raine places a crown of ribbons on Lakelyn's head.

The women coo and take photos.

Vale's not laughing though. And when our eyes meet across the room, I wish I knew what she was thinking about.

A TROUBLEMAKER

"So, HAVE YOU set a date yet?"

My aunt Helen has always been the gossip of the family. I was hoping to avoid her, but the second she saw my ring, she started grilling me for information.

I shrug and give her a little smile. "We're not sure yet. It's still very recent—the engagement. Sort of a whirlwind, you know?"

She nods. "Where will you be living?"

"I—"

"And where will the wedding be? Will you come

home for it?"

I wish I knew how to tell her I haven't considered this my home in years. At the same time, I wish I understood why it feels so natural, being here again. Like falling right back into old patterns, old routines.

"We're not sure yet." I nod toward Lakelyn. "Besides, this weekend is all about my sister and AJ."

That seems to placate her—for now.

"Vale, sweetheart." No sooner am I free of Helen than my grandmother comes over, looking frailer than I remember.

The thing about being away from home for years is holding the image of the way things and people used to be in your mind. You forget—or at least I did—that everyone gets older along with you.

Grandma's mind is still as sharp as a tack though, and her blue eyes sparkle as she waves for me to bend down a little. It's loud in here, and she wants to make sure I hear her.

"What a hunk of a man you managed to land for yourself," she whispers, elbowing me.

"Grandma!" I almost choke on my laughter.

"If only I were younger," she sighs, looking across the room.

Carter is chatting with Blake, and I can only imagine the stories Blake is telling him.

"Hey, I landed myself a hunk of a man as well when I was young. Your grandfather was considered the catch of the county. I hope the two of you are as compatible as we were. In and out of the bedroom."

Oh my God. "Uh, thank you."

"Just let me know if you need any pointers, my dear." She pats my hand. "Though if you manage to keep a man like him happy enough that he asks you to marry him with a ring like that to seal the deal, it seems you're doing just fine without my help. Must run in the family."

I honestly don't know what to do with this woman. "Now, Grandma, you know I'm a good girl."

"Mmhmm." She smirks. "I'll bet you're good."

"Shh!" I can't help but giggle. "I don't want Mom to hear."

"Don't let yourself be fooled," she warns me. "Have you ever done the math between your parents' anniversary and your eldest sister's birthday, my dear?"

"Uh, no. They were married in May, right?"

She nods. "And Brooke was born in …"

"October."

"October of the same year." She winks. "Your sister wasn't born premature either. Thought you might find that interesting." She starts off toward the other side of the barn.

Well, I'll be damned. Mom was pregnant when they got married.

I don't know if I want to laugh or cry that I never put it together.

"You're a troublemaker," I call out after her.

"What else is there to do when you get to be my age but stir up a little trouble?" she asks over her shoulder.

CHAPTER SEVEN

CONSIDER YOURSELF LUCKY.

Carter

I FIND AJ carrying gifts out to his truck while the ladies sip on champagne. "Let me help you," I offer, picking up a stand mixer and following him outside.

"Thanks. Now, we need a house just to hold all this." He scratches his head, looking at the haul in the back of the dual cab.

"Where are you storing all of this now?"

"My parents' house. In the bedroom that used to be mine. Now, I'm wondering if we should have rented storage space."

"You're lucky to have all this support."

"No doubt."

We head back to the barn for more gifts.

"Congratulations on all the exciting things happening in your life. I hear Lakelyn's a great girl."

"The best." There's no doubt that he's completely in love. You can tell just by looking at him.

His goofy expression changes, replaced by widening eyes. "I know there are a ton of great athletes that are going into the draft this year. Did you know that your office called me? Said you were interested in representing me."

"I would never have my office call a prospective client, AJ. I reached out to you personally. I was told by a man who identified himself as your father that you already had representation."

He frowns and scuffs the ground with his boot. "My representation is my uncle. He says I don't need an agent. That he knows contracts."

And he looks concerned about that. As he should be. I also get the feeling there is no one in his life besides Lakelyn who he can talk to about all this.

"What kind of contracts does he do?" I ask.

"Oh, you know, partnerships, S-corps, divorces. That kind of thing."

"So, family law? Small business? That's a broad array of specialties."

"He's pretty much the only lawyer in town."

"I see. He has to be a jack of all trades."

"Something like that. He doesn't think I need an agent, and I see his point. I could save a lot of money without one. Which could mean a lot of money if I go top five."

"That's true. What would your uncle charge you?"

"Just his normal fee for a contract review. I think it's around two fifty an hour."

I could choke. This kid has no idea what he's getting into. "What's your dad say? What about your coach?"

"My parents are super supportive. They made me what I am. But I think part of them wishes I could settle down here and start a family. They're behind me though, just like always. I chose to go to a school close by, so they could afford to come to my games, and they never missed one. But that will change when I turn pro."

"Consider yourself lucky. Many draftees are, at this very moment, surrounded by family and friends who only want a slice of the draft pie."

"I know." He scrubs a hand through his hair with a dazed grin. "It's like I dreamed of this. But I don't think anyone else other than Lakelyn thought I would actually do it."

"Even though your parents are supportive?"

He lifts a shoulder. "My parents wanted me to excel academically. Not through sports. Dad played high school football and had a scholarship to play at Arkansas. Then, he broke his leg in a car accident. The offer was rescinded, and he couldn't afford to go.

"So, my parents preached the importance of a good education. I had to keep my grades up if I wanted to stay in sports. Study, good grades, no girls. No partying."

"And did that work?"

"Hell no." We both laugh. "Nah, my freshman year was a blur of girls, working out, and hangovers. But when I got a C in a class, that was my wakeup call. Since then, it's been straight As, and no crazy partying."

"It sounds like you've got a good head on your shoulders."

"I've got good people in my corner. Like Lakelyn. She's a finance major."

"And how does she feel about your career?"

"She's fully supportive. Of course she worries I could get hurt, but she says that's why we both got our degrees. She wants to work wherever we go and plans on investing pretty much everything I earn since we don't know how long of a career I will have."

"She sounds like a keeper."

"Thus why you're here."

"It is your wedding after all." I grin.

He doesn't grin with me. "I think maybe there's another reason you're here though."

"There is. I'm incredibly in love with Vale." The words flow so easily out of my mouth, and they shock me, but fortunately, AJ doesn't seem to notice.

"Lakelyn suggested I call you to seek representation months ago. Now, she thinks you being here is the universe's way of saying that I should sign with you."

"Did she research agents?"

AJ laughs. "Not exactly. She maybe sorta has a crush on Danny Diamond and has followed his career. She read you two are close. That you are even his son's godfather."

"That is an honor, for sure. His son, Damon, is already one hell of a ballplayer. And Danny is a good father. A good man. And that combination makes it easy for me to get him lucrative endorsement deals."

AJ's eyes light up. "That's what I want. Endorsement deals. That's what my uncle can't do for me. Listen, I know I'm a decent-looking guy. I'm soon-to-be married. I even took some acting classes when I was a kid, and I was a natural in front of the camera."

He's a smart kid. He knows what brands look for and knows he fits the bill. He deserves better than some jack-of-all-trades relative handling negotiations that could affect his entire life.

"That's the part of the process I don't understand," he continues. "Do they come to me? Can I do it myself? Or do they go to guys with agents?"

"Agents facilitate things like that along the line. We constantly work with vendors to find the right fit, and I often pitch deals to them on behalf of my clients." Then, because I'm trying to be fair, I say, "It's something you could do yourself. Contact them."

"But I really won't have time, will I? I'll be training and focused."

"That's how most of my clients view it all. Yes."

He looks me up and down. "I've heard you do more for your clients. You take care of them. That it's not just about the money with you. Like with Danny. Your friendship speaks volumes."

"Here's the deal, AJ. It is about the money because we all have to make a living. But for me, it's more than that. I develop close, personal relationships with my clients. It's just how I'm wired. And I've been successful enough that I'm able to choose who I want to work with."

"I heard a rumor you turned down repping a Heisman winner because of his partying a few years ago. And that guy went first in the draft."

I nod. "And how did that turn out?"

"He crashed and burned, lost his contract. Needs rehab."

"I want to work with athletes who are serious about their careers because they get a lot of personal attention. For example, my clients work with my team of financial advisors and accountants. I don't make money off any of that, but it's important for me to know my players are in good hands. We help set up transitions for new draft picks and trades. Help them get settled into their new town, find them a home, the best schools when it comes time for stuff like that."

His eyes are almost perfectly round. "Wow."

"It's what I do." I shrug. "And there are other

things to negotiate. The contract is pretty much what it is. But we can negotiate how long it's for and how much is guaranteed income. We can talk to teams in advance and get them pumped up about you too. It looks like the first five picks this year will be Jacksonville, New York, Miami, Atlanta, and Cincinnati. Do you have a preference?"

"Really, we think we'd be happy anywhere, but I'm not a fan of cold weather. It would be fun to live somewhere warmer." He blows out a long breath through pursed lips. "You've given me a lot to think about."

"It's a big decision."

"I have a question for you. Would you even consider taking me on as a client? I mean, we'll be family. Would that complicate things?"

I love that he says we'll be *family*. That's how I want my clients to feel, but then I realize he's talking about me marrying Vale. He thinks we'll be family for real.

I clear my throat. "I believe we could keep it professional."

He nods. "My dad wouldn't be happy."

"Here's the thing, AJ, and this is important. You're not some kid anymore. You're an adult. A college graduate. You're about to be married. It's great to get advice from people you respect, like your dad and your bride, but ultimately, you—and only you—are responsible for your decisions. Your actions. You're focused on trying to decide who to please—your dad or your bride. This is your life. You should take into consideration what *you* want."

A DOORMAT

Vale

"IT LOOKS LIKE they're getting along well." Lakelyn nods toward the truck, where AJ and Carter are chatting. "I know it's not fair of him to ask for free advice and all."

"It's fine," I tell her. "I'm sure Carter doesn't mind."

"And he'll be family soon," she says.

"Yeah," I reply, feeling really bad about lying to her. She's so bright-eyed and happy right now.

"Do you think Carter would consider taking AJ on as a client? Nothing would make me happier." She leans against me, and I wrap an arm around her shoulders. It does something for my soul, standing with her like this.

How much have I missed out on, just because I can't get along with my father?

"It will all work out, Lakelyn. AJ loves you and values your opinion. The opposite of Mom and Dad, in other words. Mom would never stand up to Dad. I really don't understand it. And our sisters seem to be following that same path with their husbands." I glance over to where our mother is currently talking with the wedding planner. "Their relationship is why I have never wanted to get married," I confess.

"What?" Her head pops up off my shoulder. "Are you serious?"

"Yeah. Mom is smart, organized, and has the ability to run a large household while being a pillar of the community. She's the backbone of so many charities and organizations, yet Dad treats her like … well, the help sometimes. All that seems to matter to him is that his supper is ready at the end of their long days. I've never understood it. All I know is that I have no intention of ever living that kind of life. I don't know. Girl power and all that, but I don't want to come in second to a man. I want a partnership."

"I actually think they are a good team," Lakelyn says, tilting her head at me, like she doesn't understand why I would say such a thing. "There's a reason Dad always takes her along to his business dinners. And not just because wives are usually included and everyone knows everyone."

"What do you mean?"

"While you seem to picture her as some kind of doormat, I see her as a complement to him. They balance each other out. She's his softer side. He speaks before he thinks. She brings things back around and keeps the conversation flowing and positive."

"How do you know?"

"She told me so once. I asked why she always goes with him. I figured it would be boring, you know. She said he needs her there. She's the people person. He's the one with business sense. She also says that sometimes, when you are married to a strong man with strong opinions, you have to pick your battles. And when something is meaningful to her, she does."

"Really?" I ask, feeling stunned.

"Yeah. And I get it. AJ and I have very different personalities, and we can bring out the best in each other, using our strengths to be stronger as a whole."

Her words make me see my parents' relationship in a different light, but I don't have time to think about that now because she quickly switches gears.

"Can you even believe tonight is our bachelor and bachelorette parties?" Her eyebrows move up and down, suggestive and playful.

I can tell she's dying to know what we're doing, so I decide to egg her on a little. "I wonder *whatever* we will do with ourselves tonight. You know, when I was planning it all out, I thought, *What would Lakelyn want?* And I knew it would have to be a super-low-key night. Just some girl bonding. Maybe a few beers out by the firepit. I told the girls to all bring comfy clothes."

"Really?" she says, looking a combination of disappointed and not wanting to hurt my feelings. "I kinda bought a party dress."

"I maybe kinda bought a party dress too," I say with a laugh. "It's a surprise."

"Honestly, as long as I can wear my dress and hang with my girls, I'll be happy."

"Then, you will most definitely have fun tonight! What are the guys doing?"

"I'm not sure. All I know is that BTO and Blake planned it and said it was going to be a wild night. And even though I totally trust AJ, you know how they are. They both push others to do stupid things. And that worries me a little."

I give her another hug. "You don't have to worry. Carter will keep an eye on him. He wouldn't let AJ do something stupid right before the draft."

"I'm sure glad he's here," she says.

And when I look over at Carter, I have to agree.

CHAPTER EIGHT
PROCEED WITH CAUTION.

Carter

"DO YOU HAVE any idea what I might be in for later tonight?"

Vale sighs, her eyes meeting mine in the mirror as she brushes her hair, getting ready. "There's a strip club just north of town, and Trent and Blake like to go there. And although Lakelyn trusts AJ, she's worried the boys will get him drunk and do something stupid."

"The notion of a top draft pick partying at a strip club with those two is a recipe for disaster. Bachelor party or not. When you've seen as many innocent nights go south as I have, trust me, you know the signs."

She turns to me, leaning against the dresser with her arms folded under her chest. Her dress is low-cut in the front, and I'm having a hard time focusing on anything else. If we were together for real, I would grab her and throw her onto the bed this second.

Vale gives me her supermodel smile and says

sexily, "I know he's not your client, but is there any chance you would watch out for him tonight? Make sure he doesn't get himself into any trouble? And keep an eye on Blake while you're at it."

"He's a hell-raiser, isn't he?"

"Something tells me that my brother and Trent have been looking forward to tonight ever since the engagement was announced." She pauses and taps a slender finger against her bottom lip. "I could see them trying to get AJ really drunk. Almost hazing him. All in the name of good fun, of course."

"I'll make a note of that." I close my eyes and rub my temples in hopes of warding off a headache as I take a seat on the side of the little bed we're both expected to sleep in. I shouldn't be thinking about it so much. About how close I'll be to her. Back in college, a twin dorm bed was plenty of room for two, and this bed is much bigger than that. "I'm starting to feel too old for this shit. I'm an agent, not a babysitter, which is why I'm picky about the type of man I take on as a client. But whether or not AJ becomes my client doesn't matter. I like the guy, and I'm not going to let his stupid friends ruin his life."

She walks up next to me and puts her hands on my shoulders. "Thank you, Carter. I can tell this is stressing you out. And I'm sorry it is. But for what it's worth, I'm really glad you're here with me."

Which is a really nice thing to say, but then she massages my shoulders. It's something she would do before. It's something I loved. But today, it makes me flinch.

Which causes her to pull her hands off me immediately. I can tell by the look on her face that she thinks I don't want her to touch me because I don't care about her, but she's wrong. I flinch because I seriously don't know if I trust myself with her. My thoughts are filled with sex. With desire. With love.

But I can't say that.

So, I go with something less volatile. "And to think, my plans for today included a jog on the beach, a few hours of work, and Mexican food and margaritas with my sister. Then, you showed up at my door."

"Oh, come on," she says, taking a seat next to me. "Don't act like you've never had unexpected excitement throw your day off course."

"Make that a four-day weekend," I counter.

This I can do. Be flirty, playful. It comes natural. But then so do a whole lot of other things with her.

I need to get off this bed.

But I stay seated.

"I do really appreciate you being here, Carter."

She lightly runs her fingers down the inside of my arm. Another one of her ways to relax me. The good news is, it does release some of the tension. The bad news is that the blood in my body is now focusing on a different area below my belt.

"Did you really think that I wouldn't do this for

you? Regardless of what happened with our relationship, I will always care for you." Thus the reason that ring is on her finger right now. I couldn't possibly get rid of it. I couldn't tear it apart and sell the diamonds like they were nothing more than scraps.

She lets out a sad laugh. "Do you mean that?"

Our gazes meet and hold tight. I just stare into her beautiful eyes.

Then, I smirk at her. "Besides, you were on your knees. What man could turn that down?"

She smiles at me and kisses me on the cheek. "I was desperate. It's kind of embarrassing."

"I came here willingly. Even if the situation is totally fucked up."

"Welcome to my life," she says with a sigh but follows it up with a chuckle.

"I miss your life," I blurt out.

"What do you mean?"

"I miss you in my life. Do you think when we go back to California, we could be friends? Hang out a little?" God, I sound desperate. Of course, sitting next to her, I most definitely am.

"You mean, like, we'll hook up?"

And the way her face brightens at the thought is like a punch to the gut. The little reality check that I needed. That's all I ever was to her and all I'll ever be.

I let out the kind of dramatic sigh my sister, Chloe, usually makes. "No, I just mean, be friends."

"I think I could handle that," she says then adds, "You know, my family already adores you."

"And I hate lying to them about us. But here we are. At least your grandma gives good hugs," I tease.

Vale grins but looks like she's trying to hold back her laughter. "Yes, well, she is affectionate."

I decide to break her composure. "She grabbed my ass."

Laughter bursts from her mouth. And it's contagious. I can't help but laugh with her and pull her down on the bed with me.

Both of us are lying on our backs, laughing hysterically. It's fun, and it makes it almost possible to forget why I'm here.

How this is all an act.

But I might as well enjoy it while it lasts.

I turn to face her as she continues to giggle. "She asked if my grandfather is still alive."

"She did not!" Vale giggles some more, covering her mouth with her hand, trying to stifle it. It's the cutest thing ever. "Do I need to have a talk with her?"

I suggestively put my hand on her hip and smile at her. "I think I can handle it."

"You going to handle things in the strip club tonight?" she sasses back.

It's another thing I love about her. She can give shit as much as she can take it. When she drapes her arm over my shoulder and moves closer to me, I become very serious. Especially when her voice drops in pitch and her breath feels warm against my ear.

"You in the mood for a lap dance?"

The air leaves my chest. And although my brain knows she's just joking around, my body isn't having it.

Because all I can think about is stripping off her dress.

It's often what I used to do the second she walked through my door. Half the time, we never made it to the bedroom. She'd call, say she was in town. I'd tell her to stop by. We both knew what that meant. Whether it was for a night or a few days, they would be filled with amazing sex.

Part of me wishes that's all it had been. That I hadn't fallen for her.

"From you? Yes." My hand moves from her hip to her chest, grazing its way across her cleavage. "This is a nice dress."

"You're staring at my cleavage like you've never seen it before. You've seen me in a lot less than this, Carter."

"The *less* is exactly what I'm thinking about."

"Really?"

"Really. You're beautiful, Vale. But I'm sure everyone tells you that."

"Not you. Not in a while."

"Yeah, well," I say, realizing the path we are headed down. A hot hook-up right here in her room.

I stand up just as the door to the bedroom is thrown open.

"Vale, your mother is looking for you," Trent says, but he stops dead in his tracks, seeing how Vale is suggestively sprawled out on the bed.

"Don't you know how to knock?" I ask him.

He just gives me a shrug. "Sorry. Old habits and all."

What the hell is that supposed to mean?

Before I have the chance to ask her, Vale gets up and says, "Thanks for the heads-up, Trent."

I want to say something to her. I need to say something to her, but instead, I let her just breeze past me and out the door.

Probably out of my life.

Again.

I finish getting dressed and then sneak down the back stairs and outside to get better cell reception and so I can hopefully talk without anyone overhearing me.

I find a secluded garden bench, take a seat, and then stare at my phone, wondering who to call as a conversation from the past rolls through my brain. Our family trip to Palmilla. Sitting outside, talking to my older brother, Cade.

"So, what's the deal with Vale?" he asked me.

"We hook up. It's fantastic, but it's supposed to just be fun. Nothing serious."

"But you want more than that?"

I ran my hand through my hair in frustration. "She travels a lot. Says she doesn't want to be in a serious relationship, but when we're together, it feels like it could be serious."

And it still feels that way.

"How did you meet her again?"

"Super Bowl party last year. We got teamed up in a video game contest. She beat me."

"Did you let her win?"

"No, I just … she was beautiful, you know. It was hard to concentrate."

"Fell hard fast?"

"Pretty girls don't fluster me," I said. "But she sure did. She's beautiful and all, but she's cute too."

"The girl every boy wishes they could have grown up next door to."

"I would have been spanking it every day. It would have been torture," I said with a laugh.

"Oh, give me a break," he replied, slapping me on the back. "The quarterback always gets the girl."

"I'm not the quarterback anymore. It's weird how your life changes. I thought for sure I'd be playing pro ball now. It was all I worked toward, growing up."

"You used to tell us you were going to be on TV every Sunday."

"Until the injury that ended my career."

"Yeah, well, when they carted you off on a back-

board, none of us were worried about your career, Carter. We were worried about your life. It was a violent collision that broke your back in three places. You're lucky you weren't paralyzed."

"I know. Life has worked out well for me regardless. I love being a sports agent. I've done very well, so it's not that I'm complaining really, but part of me wonders if I were, if Vale would fall for me."

"If she would fall for you just because you were a professional quarterback, you shouldn't want her," he said firmly.

"I know."

"Have you told her how you feel?"

"No. I don't want to mess up a good thing. Or scare her away."

"If you love her, Carter, you should tell her."

"I feel like I'm on the scout team with her."

"And you want to be the starter?"

"Yeah," I admitted.

"Is she seeing other people? Are you?"

"In the last month, I haven't. I don't know about her. She's been traveling nonstop since New York Fashion Week. We talk almost every day, but she could have a different guy in every country for all I know."

"When you see her tomorrow, you should ask her."

"Maybe."

"You aren't going to, are you?"

"No, not yet. I don't want to screw things up."

"Do you ever think about getting married?" he

asked me.

I knew it was on his mind. He had recently seen Palmer Montlake at a wedding. Cade and her brother Pike had been best friends and teammates, growing up, and when Palmer and Cade had secretly dated and then broken up, he'd not only lost the love of his life, but he'd lost his best friend too.

"Our brother is certainly happy," I said, glancing at our youngest brother, Cash, and his new wife, Ashlyn, who were wrapped in each other's arms, kissing.

"Cash was always a serial dater," Cade said. "Unlike you."

I couldn't help but grin and recall my glory days. "I did get a lot of tail in college."

"One of the benefits of being a star collegiate quarterback."

"Or the star catcher," I reminded him. "Remember those shirts all the girls wore when you and Pike were playing together? When I was in high school, my goal in life was to someday have stands full of girls wearing my name."

"The I got Piked *shirts?"*

"If I recall, many said, Caught by Cade.*"*

"Well, back then, there was a lot of juggling on the lineup." He took a pull of his beer and laughed.

"Seems like there's still a lot of juggling on the lineup for you. Be honest with me." I asked seriously, "Do you wish you were hitting home runs with the same girl every night?"

We both glanced at the house. Ashlyn was now lying on the couch with her head in Cash's lap. He was gently stroking her hair as they talked.

"They do look happy," he admitted.

"After Cash and his longtime girlfriend broke up, he was a lot like us, playing the field," I stated. "Until he met Ashlyn."

"Exactly my point," Cade said. "You never know when it will hit you. He went to a wedding, hoping to get laid, and now, look at him."

"So, you're saying, there's hope for me and Vale?"

"I'm saying, you never know."

"She's like a guy when it comes to sex. I'm not quite sure how to handle her," I said.

And I realize I'm still not sure.

I could call Cade, but he and Palmer are expecting their first child and are deliriously happy. And they never started as a hook-up. My brother Cash and his wife, Ashlyn, however did. They got drunk together, flew to Vegas on my plane, had a wild night, and ended up married. It's the kind of night an agent prays one of their clients never has. Ashlyn didn't even know Cash's real name or that he was our younger brother.

But the truth is, sometimes, fate does play a role in life because they are perfect for each other.

And honestly, that's why I'm sitting in a garden in Iowa, pretending to be the fiancé of the girl I wanted to marry at her little sister's wedding.

Because of the off chance that this is fate's way of intervening in my life.

I close my eyes and dial the number, feeling relieved when Ashlyn answers.

"Hey, Carter," she says. "What's up?"

"A lot actually. Are you busy? Do you have a minute to talk? Is Cash sitting right next to you?"

"That's a lot of questions. I happen to be on set, waiting for my next scene. Yes, I have a minute. Actually, I have ten. And, no, Cash is at work. Where are you?"

"Iowa. Possibly in the middle of a cornfield."

She lets out a laugh. "It's funny that you called. I've been thinking of you a lot today."

"Why's that?"

"The role I'm playing. Remember how Cade tried to set us up before I met Cash?"

I can't help but laugh. "I thought you were hot, but we had no sparks."

"Exactly. Isn't that weird? You were totally my type. Former college quarterback, smart, had a great body. You're sweet and sexy. So, the question is, why? Why didn't we connect? Why didn't we just hook up?"

"Because you were meant to be with my brother," I say.

"And that's what makes it even weirder, right? It's like fate knew or something that I shouldn't be with you because if I had, it probably wouldn't have worked out for me and Cash, and then I'd be sad instead of stupid happy with your brother."

"And that is exactly why I'm calling. Because you believe in that stuff."

"Wait. Vale is from Iowa."

"Yep. She showed up on my doorstep this morning. Begged me to come with her to her little sister's wedding."

"But you haven't seen her in months. And you've never told us what really happened between you two."

"That's because it's embarrassing."

"You've known me a long time, Carter. You know plenty of embarrassing things about me."

I laugh. "True. Okay, so I flew to New York on New Year's Eve for her party. I'd told her I didn't know if I would be able to be there because I wanted to surprise her."

"Oh, Carter," Ashlyn says slowly, clearly understanding. "Let me guess. You got surprised instead?"

"Yeah. The weather and traffic were horrible. I barely made it in time before the clock hit midnight. And I saw her kissing another man. I was going to propose, Ash."

"She told me you didn't show up."

"That's because I didn't tell her the truth. Why would I?"

"She also told me that you said as the clock

struck midnight, you realized she wasn't the girl for you. You broke her heart."

"Well, she broke mine first. And have you been talking to her about me?"

"Yes, occasionally. We're friends, Carter. When you said what you did, she assumed that there was someone else."

"There wasn't for me, but obviously, there was for her. I'm glad I saw that before I stupidly proposed."

"And why are you calling me now?"

"Because I'm pretending to be her fake fiancé."

"You're what?!"

"Yes, I have to lie to her family and pretend to love her."

"But you're not pretending," she says astutely.

"I agreed to this whole mess because I do still love her, and I called you because of your feelings on fate. What I need to know is if this is fate's way of bringing her back in my life. I had to do this, right? Just in case it is. I feel like I'm either crazy or an idiot."

"That's love for you," Ashlyn says with a laugh. "And for what it's worth, I do believe fate *has* given you a second chance. You need to tell her what you did. What you saw. And how you felt. And you need to really pay attention to how she responds." She's quiet for a moment before adding, "Carter, you give good advice. Always. What advice would you give to yourself in this situation?"

"I would tell myself to follow my heart and go get my girl."

"Then, do it. And for goodness' sake, text me and keep me updated. I'd better not have to wait until the weekend is over to hear how it went."

"Don't tell the family, okay?" I beg. "Not yet."

She laughs. "You picked the wrong girl to call, Carter. I can't keep a secret to save my life. You should have called Cade for that."

"Fuck," I mutter under my breath as I end the call.

ANOTHER WEDDING.

Vale

"Sorry about that," Trent says to me. "I didn't mean to cause trouble."

I can't help but shoot him a dirty look. "Yes, you did. You forget how well I know you."

"*Knew* me. Been a long time since you have been back home."

"Well, some things don't change. Are you still in the habit of walking around the house like you own the place?"

"Yeah, sort of," he admits. "This has always been my second home. Your mom still has me over for Sunday dinner."

"She does not," I gasp.

He turns to me, lifting his broad shoulders. "What's the matter with that?"

Does he really want to know?

"What about … you know, a girlfriend? Don't you ever have other plans?"

"Sundays are for the Martins. As for girlfriends, there hasn't been anyone serious in a very long time."

He gives me a meaningful look that I hope doesn't mean what it seems to.

Has he really not been in a relationship since I left?

"Trent, you deserve better than that."

"With all due respect, Vale, I think I'm the best one to decide what I deserve. I know what I'm after." He winks at me before sauntering off.

And it makes me feel a little sick to my stomach.

"THERE YOU ARE," my mother says, rushing past me as she comes through the front door. "I could use another pair of hands, honey. Everyone is outside, prepping and baking the pizzas, but I need to get the sides out there."

"Pizzas?" I ask.

"Yes, that's what your sister and AJ requested for tonight's pre-party. Their favorite thing to do when they came home from college was to make all sorts of creative pizza combinations in the outdoor oven."

"You have an outdoor oven?"

"Yes, for pizza. Come. You'll see."

"Sorry I took so long upstairs. I left LA really early this morning and needed to freshen up for tonight."

I grab a platter filled with a caprese salad while she has her arms wrapped around a large wooden salad bowl, and I follow her to a beautifully constructed outdoor patio. It's situated between the main barn and the house and a new addition to the land since the last time I was here. Just as the barn is set up for parties, this is too. There are lights strung across the rafters of a pergola, hanging over a long, heavy wooden dining table—the kind that comfortably seats about twenty. Scattered about are other smaller dining tables and seating areas.

There's a line of trees near the house, most likely for both privacy and to block the chilly north winds, but the back is open to the formal garden, gazebo, and then to the rolling meadow beyond.

There's a full outdoor kitchen with dual gas grills, a smoker, and a pizza oven. Adjacent from it is a bar for serving drinks and a buffet counter. Plants add color and beauty.

Although I noticed the trees were new when I arrived, I didn't realize all this was back here.

It's like a little secret garden.

"This is beautiful," I tell my mother.

"It turned out great. One of my favorite places on the farm. The old patio we used when you were a kid got small as our family expanded. And the space is great for throwing parties. We often use it as a spot for cocktails before hosting benefits in the barn. Your father is a pillar of the community. I really wish you didn't butt heads. Have you spoken to him yet?"

"A little."

"Vale." She gives me a stern look.

"What am I supposed to talk to him about? He was downright rude to Carter when we arrived, and I don't want to cause a scene during my sister's wedding weekend."

Mom seems to ignore all that. "Your father likes Carter. I can tell you that much."

Funny how I can feel strangely proud and guilty as hell all at once.

"He should. Carter's a great guy."

"I hope we're all able to get to know him. And get reacquainted with you. It's been a while."

"Yes, it has. But you know why."

"Regardless, I'm happy for you, sweetheart. As soon as we get through this weekend, we'll have another wedding to plan," she says happily.

"We just got engaged," I say flippantly as we make our way back to the house and into the dining room to retrieve whatever else needs to be brought out. "I haven't had time to think about what kind of wedding I want or where I want it to be. Carter's family is all in California, and our friends are spread out all over the world."

She stops at the end of the long table and turns to face me. "You don't want to have your wedding here?" she says, sucking in a breath.

I wonder why in the world she would ever think I would want to.

"I wouldn't hold my breath on that one, Mom," my sister Brooke says, rolling her eyes. "She hasn't been home in four years, and that was only for Lakelyn's high school graduation ceremony."

I'm hoping she'll stay and back me up, but she picks up a tray of pink-frosted cupcakes and hightails it out of the house.

"It's Lakelyn's weekend—her wedding, Mom. Let's focus on that. Besides, I want to plan and pay for my own wedding."

"What's this?" my father says, his voice booming from behind us.

I swear, the man has a sixth sense. Whenever I'm talking about something he's likely to have a problem with—in other words, just about anything at all—he finds a way to overhear it.

"You too good to let your father pay for your wedding?"

Even if my mother understood why I'd want to pay and plan my own wedding, I know she won't say anything, so I say with as much patience as I can muster, "I. Haven't. Made. Any. Wedding. Plans.

Yet."

"Too good for us," my father says, nodding his head. "You always thought you were too good."

"Can we not do this right now?" I beg. "Not this weekend."

"It'll be too late to have it the next time we see each other, going by the frequency with which you come home to see your family," he says, adding insult to injury.

"I can't imagine why I don't come home more often," I say flatly, "when I get such a warm welcome and have so many of these touching, tender family moments."

CHAPTER NINE
NOT MY PROBLEM

Carter

I SNEAK IN through the back of the house and immediately can tell something's wrong. There are angry voices coming from down the hall, and I head toward them, finding myself at the entry to the kitchen.

I see a table in the center of the room, acting as both an island and a place to dine. It's much more casual than the rest of the home. Actually, that's something that has surprised me most about Vale's home. The way she spoke of the place had me thinking it would be a shabby, old farmhouse, not this beautiful and grand country home.

The kitchen is the most rustic of the rooms I've seen, but it's cozy and warm. The sort of kitchen I would expect to see on a farm, only much larger, with top-of-the-line appliances. There are herbs and flowers on the windowsills, a basket of eggs on the counter. I can imagine quiet Sunday morning breakfasts in this room, sunlight streaming in. It's really soothing here, and I can see why so many celebrities build homes like this, away from it all—to do nothing but relax with their families.

There's nothing relaxing about what is going on now though. Vale and her father are having words in the nearby dining room, and then she storms out before I can even step into the room.

"Isn't it bad enough the man couldn't speak to me before asking for my daughter's hand?" Mr. Martin says to his wife.

"Please, don't hold that against her," I say, boldly joining them. "I couldn't help myself, as I told you earlier."

At least Mrs. Martin has the grace to look embarrassed. Her husband is another matter. He smirks, folding his arms in a way that reminds me of Vale.

"We settled that, son, but now, I hear you're not going to let me pay for my daughter's wedding." He holds his arms out and gestures around him. "Is this not good enough for either of you?"

"We haven't made any plans yet, sir," I explain, glancing at his wife. "As you both know, we've been engaged for a *very* short time."

I can tell Mrs. Martin appreciates this.

She touches her husband's arm. "We don't have to talk about this now. And I shouldn't have even brought it up today. I just got carried away at the thought of helping to plan my Vale's wedding."

I do what I can to ignore the clenching of my

heart. Vale's mother seems nice. And she will be hurt when she finds out our engagement was just a sham.

Not that I had much time to think things over this morning, but it hits me like a ton of bricks now. Vale will have to tell her family of our *breakup*, and I can't help but wonder how they will take the news.

Obviously, not my problem, but still.

If I'm nothing else, I'm good in a room. I am very good at presenting myself to potential clients. But I am always honest with them. I want to be clear about my expectations upfront. In other words, I don't lie to them. I don't embellish. My father always says a man is only as good as his word.

This weekend, I'm not feeling like a good man. I hate lying. But I love Vale. And whether or not we'll ever be together doesn't matter. I agreed to do this for her.

"It's probably my fault, sir," I say, standing up tall. "I'm of the age and means that I just assumed that I would pay for our wedding. I don't mean to insult you in any way. Just know that if contributing to our day is important to you, I'm sure we can work something out."

Only then do I notice Vale standing on the other side of the room with tears in her eyes.

And I wish it didn't make me feel so good, having her look at me like that.

FINISH THIS LATER.

Vale

CARTER WALKS TOWARD me, takes my hand, and leads me outside to the porch.

I wrap my arms around his waist, glad he's here. "Thank you for what you just said. I'm sorry about this mess."

He leans closer to me, almost looking like he might kiss me. Instead, he just runs his hand through his hair. "I understand now why you don't come home much."

"Being here, even though things with my father aren't good, makes me realize all that I'm missing out on. I've only seen Sophie a few times in person and only because my sisters came to visit me."

He kisses my forehead. And it's the sweetest gesture ever.

"I'm going to kiss you now," he says. "Because I wanted to when we were laughing on the bed and I'm regretting it."

I toss my arms around his neck and press my lips against his. And, my God, does it feel good. Our lips part. Our tongues intertwine. Carter deepens the kiss.

And it's like I've been starving for him. I want to wrap my legs around his waist and never let go of him, but just as I start to, I hear a cough.

Carter stops kissing me. And I'm praying it's not my father.

Fortunately, when I open my eyes, I just find Trent on the porch with us.

Carter practically growls in my ear. And it's such a turn-on. "Don't you have some pizzas to cook, *best man*?" he says to Trent.

"I am the best man," Trent says back, but he doesn't go anywhere.

Carter kisses me again. This time, just a sweet peck. Then, he whispers to me, "We'll finish this later."

And I sincerely hope what he said is true. I want to ask him this now, but I know better. Not in front of Trent.

Instead, I just smack him playfully on the butt like I used to when we were dating and say, "I'll hold you to that." Then, I let my body sway sexily as I walk away.

DINNER IS CASUAL, and the baking of the pizzas is a fun event. Everyone is hanging out by the ovens. When a pizza is finished cooking, it gets laid out on the bar, and everyone samples a piece.

We're trying a mushroom and onion pizza with a white sauce and enjoying a couple of beers when I whisper to Carter, "You really did handle my father beautifully earlier. I appreciate it."

"I'm used to keeping a cool head in hot situations. Besides, you thanked me with your lips already." He winks at me before picking up a piece of pizza—this one sausage, spinach, and feta—and feeds me a bite. "These pizzas are damn good."

"And smart. Lots of carbs to soak up the alcohol tonight."

"So, Vale"—my aunt Helen slides up next to us with my grandmother in tow—"when are you two going to start a family?"

"Well, I plan on drinking heavily tonight, so probably not anytime too soon," I joke, wondering why they are even at the dinner before the bachelorette and bachelor parties.

Hopefully, they don't plan on coming to the bachelorette party. I didn't invite them or Mom, but now, I'm worried they will come anyway.

"Oh, honey," Helen says, patting my hand, "alcohol is usually how babies get made."

Carter chokes on his beer. And I have to stifle a laugh.

"You're not getting any younger, you know. The clock is ticking."

I really wish Carter would say something, but he's just watching with an amused look on his face.

"I'll keep that in mind. In the meantime, I have plenty of nieces and nephews to spoil."

Though I have to admit, I don't spoil them much. Other than the gifts I send whenever I see something cute, I don't have much to do with their lives at all.

That's one thing I'm missing out on. Watching them grow.

"There's still time for that," I murmur to myself.

"For what?" Carter asks as Grandma and Helen turn their attention to Blake, who is refilling their glasses with their favorite peach wine. "What were you talking about? Time for what? Kids?"

I have to keep my voice low. "To spoil my nieces and nephews."

He nods in understanding. "You haven't gotten to spend much time with them, I assume."

"I haven't, and it makes me feel so bad."

His expression softens. "You have your reasons for staying away."

"At what cost though? I'm missing so much. I almost missed all of this. I can barely believe that I nearly told my little sister that I couldn't come to her wedding."

"You're here now. That's what matters." He gently nudges me with a little smile. "You're going to make a lot of happy memories this weekend. Don't let your tenuous relationship with your father get in the way of that."

Happy memories.

Aside from witnessing Lakelyn's wedding, I wonder how many happy memories I'll be able to take with me after this weekend is over.

And how many of them will include Carter?

Grandma and Helen are back at our side. Plates and glasses refilled.

"I just love seeing the two of you together." My grandmother is wearing what can only be described as a shit-eating grin. "You're such a pretty couple."

"Thank you." I take Carter's arm, pulling him closer to me, partially to protect him from these women, who seem to lose all their decorum around him. "I mean, I think *he's* the one who got lucky, but …"

"I know I am." Carter pats my hand as he gives my grandmother a wide grin, the one packed so full of cockiness that he could charm the panties off any woman in the room.

At least, it always worked on me.

"Do me a favor, sweetheart," Grandma coos, nudging me. "Give him a kiss for me. Really lay one on him."

I know we kissed on the porch, but that was in private. And I don't even know what it meant.

Besides, Carter's not a show dog. I can't expect him to just act on command.

"Uh, I'm a little shy when it comes to public displays of affection," I reply hazily, not even sure what I just said made sense. Because I'm still lost in a memory of a particularly passionate night in New York City during Fashion Week. We'd been at the club, dancing close all night. Drinking. Grinding on each other. It was like four straight hours of foreplay, and when we got back to our room—

"Honey," Helen says, "you flash your rear end and bosom all over the world on a regular basis. And those pictures are blown up and put on billboards. I hardly doubt a simple kiss from your man could be considered indecent."

Grandma nods in agreement.

And they have a point.

I glance at Carter.

He grins at me in a way that lets me know he's game for it, but he teases Grandma and Helen anyway. "I don't flash my rear end and bosom though," he offers.

Helen rolls her eyes and says, "Youth is wasted on the young," while Grandma leans over and squeezes Carter's bicep.

Mom joins us. "Are you two causing trouble again?" she asks Grandma.

"No, Sarah, we are not. And I would thank you to speak to your mother with a little respect."

"Yes, ma'am," Mom murmurs with a wink my way.

"We wanted to see these two kiss, is all." Grandma pouts. "It makes me happy to see Vale in love. I mean, I might not live to see the wedding."

"Grandma!" I gasp.

"It would do an old lady's heart good to see her favorite, most beautiful granddaughter kiss her handsome beau. Is that such a crime?"

CHAPTER TEN
FAIR WARNING.

Carter

I SAY NO matter how old Grandma is, she needs to get laid. I've never met anyone so determined to watch a kiss.

And after the kiss earlier, I'm more than happy to oblige.

So, I do what the old woman wants. I place my hands on Vale's waist and try not to think about other times when I've pulled her to me like this.

It doesn't work.

She rests her hands on my chest and tips her head back, her lips waiting.

Soft. Sweet. Lips I still crave.

It's safe to say that the kiss on the porch didn't cure me of my addiction. If anything, I just want to kiss her more. But I need to stay in control.

I lower my head and plant a respectable kiss on Vale's lips.

"Pooh."

That clearly wasn't good enough for Grandma.

With a dry laugh, I shrug. "Hey, that's as frisky as I get in front of family. Have you met her father?"

Vale's eyes open, and I wish I knew what was going on behind them.

What is she thinking? Why am I putting myself through this torture if I mean nothing to her?

Vale giggles nervously as I think about how we kissed a few moments ago and her reaction, but then a vision of the guy making out with her on New Year's Eve flashes in my brain, giving me a whiplash of emotion.

"If you ladies will excuse me, I have some things to discuss with Blake and the others. Bachelor party things." I make a funny face that causes Grandma to laugh.

But the moment I turn away from them, I stop smiling. This playing the happy couple and navigating the family dynamics is difficult enough without all my old feelings resurfacing.

It would probably be easier if I could just hate her.

Trent surprises me by handing me a cold beer. "Tonight should be interesting," he says.

I take the beer from him instead of smashing the bottle over his head like I would have liked to do when he interrupted our porch kiss. But since I need to get through the bachelor party for AJ's sake, I act civil. "I heard Blake say you boys have big plans for AJ tonight."

"Yeah. Limo, drinks, strip club—the works."

"I'd love to pitch in. I know I'm a last-minute addition."

He waves a hand. "No worries." But then he gives me a staredown. Apparently sizing up what he thinks is his competition.

If he only knew.

"So, you and Vale, huh?"

"I'm a lucky guy," I lie.

"Fair warning." He leans in like we're BFFs and he's about to tell me a secret. "Blake intends to test you out tonight. See the sort of guy you really are. Whether you're good enough for his sister."

I can't help but laugh. "I would do the same to any man who managed to catch my sister's attention, so I can't blame him," I lie again. I would never disrespect my sister in that way. "I know you're close to the Martins. Is that how you and AJ became so close?"

"He practically grew up in this house, like me," Trent says with a chuckle. "He's a great kid. Good head on his shoulders."

I notice Trent wince. "You okay?"

"Yeah." He pats his stomach. "Too much celebrating. Gotta keep in mind, I'm not a young buck anymore."

"You'd better pace yourself if you want to hang with the college boys tonight," I warn him.

All I know is that I want him wherever Vale isn't.

I don't like the way his eyes linger on her, and I certainly don't like the way he brags about practically growing up in her house.

It feels like the one-up game. Like because he's known her longer, she should be his by default.

Sorry, dude.

Although I know their past is none of my business.

And I shouldn't be jealous.

But I can't stop thinking about that kiss—and I'm *not* talking about the one in front of Grandma.

MAYBE I'LL GET LUCKY.

"WHO ARE YOU talking to?" Lakelyn asks, catching me as I'm getting off the phone.

"Huh? Me?" I touch a hand to my chest. "Why would you care? Do you think I'm up to something? Like your bachelorette party perhaps?"

"You have been acting sneaky. Brooke and Raine are staying close-lipped about tonight, which means you told them to keep their mouths shut."

"At least they're doing what I asked—for once. But you aren't that big on surprises, are you?"

"I love surprises," she counters. "I just like to have an *idea* of the surprise, so I can prepare for it."

"If you can prepare for it, it's not a surprise."

"Can't you just tell me a little something? I'll be honest. I'm a little worried about tonight. I know the boys are doing the strip-club thing, but that's not really my style."

"I know that. And even though it was highly suggested that we go to a male revue, I had something different in mind. Something fun. More interactive than just sitting and watching guys dance."

She lets out a relieved sigh. "How should I dress? I bought a few different options."

"Short, sexy. Cute. I'll take care of the rest."

She throws herself in my arms. "I'm really glad you're here. Promise me that when I move, we'll spend more time together. That you'll come to some of AJ's games. See my new home. I love and miss you. And it's high time we stopped letting Dad interfere in our relationship, don't you think?"

I hug her tightly as tears fill my eyes. "Definitely time, and I promise. Now," I say, untangling myself and turning her toward the house, "let's go get all glammed up. Do you want me to do your makeup?"

"I would love that," she says.

I meet her in her room after grabbing my makeup kit. I might have hoped that would be her answer. I brought some false eyelashes with pink feathers mixed in that will be super fun if she can wear them and still manage to see.

She pulls three dresses out of her closet. The first is a tight black party dress, the second is a nude-colored jumpsuit with a bandeau top covered with tiny pastel rhinestones, and the third is a beaded and sequined fitted party dress. "What do you think?"

"Which is your favorite?"

"Well, I love them all, but I was thinking pink for tonight and the jumpsuit for the rehearsal."

"What's the black dress for?"

"In case we went to see male dancers. I didn't want anything that would show dirt."

This makes me laugh.

I do up her makeup, pretty and pink, subtle mostly, except for the lashes, and then I turn her toward the mirror. "What do you think?"

She flutters her eyes like she was born with ridiculously long lashes and squeals. "I loooove them!" She preens in the mirror some more. Then, she looks at me. "Why don't I curl my own hair while you go get yourself ready? We're meeting at ten, right?"

"Yep, we need to be downstairs then."

I start to leave her room but then turn around and say, "Is it true Trent is still having dinner here on Sundays?" Because part of me wonders if he's telling the truth.

"There's always a spot for him at the table, for sure," she says. "I don't know about every Sunday since I've been away at college, but he's always here when AJ and I are."

The way she replies is so straightforward. Like it's normal. No big deal. But then again, his family life wasn't great when we were in high school. His dad left, and maybe my dad stepped in to fill the role.

"Plus, he works at the car dealership with Jake now. So, he's practically family."

"Is it just me, or is it kind of weird?"

She rolls her eyes. "Everyone knows he's always carried a torch for you. I swear, I don't know what power you have over men, but I would've killed for some of it back in the day."

"You've always had AJ wrapped around your finger."

"Still, there's a time in every girl's life when she wouldn't mind leaving men panting after her. When he broke up with me freshman year, I thought we were over forever." She studies my face. "What's wrong?"

"It seems like Trent hasn't moved on," I admit. "And I don't like the way he looks at me."

"There have always been extra people for Sunday dinner. Come on. Don't worry about it. I think it's really good for Trent to see how crazy in love you are with Carter. I mean, it's written all over your face every time you look at him. Maybe this will give Trent some closure. Who knows? Maybe he'll get lucky tonight."

"What do you mean?"

"He could meet a stripper and fall in love." Lakelyn grins at me before shooing me out the door.

CHAPTER ELEVEN
VISCOUSLY SEXY.

Carter

"ARE YOU EXCITED for tonight?" I ask Vale when she comes into the bedroom.

I'm lying on the bed, relaxing. Actually, that's not true. I've been thinking about having sex with Vale. On this bed.

"I am. My sisters told me we needed to go see male dancers. I didn't think Lakelyn would love that. So, I got a limo and some fun props, and we're going to make a game out of barhopping," she says, throwing open her closet.

Earlier today, she hung a viciously sexy party dress up to get the wrinkles out, and now, she's stripping off her clothes, presumably going to change into it. She's used to changing in front of a lot of people at fashion shows, but I'm not a lot of people.

Her back is to me, and it's like she's trying to be modest. In front of me. Who has seen every part of her in intimate detail.

She reaches behind her and unhooks her bra, and

even though I can't see them, I can picture her breasts perfectly. I know exactly what they look like—

"Hello?" She glances over her shoulder. "Earth to Carter."

"Huh?" Damn it, I need a cold shower. Probably several of them.

"I know you're worried about AJ tonight. I just asked if you were worried about me getting in trouble. You know, I used to be a bit of a hell-raiser myself, back in the day."

This makes me laugh and shake my head. "I just can't picture it. I can't imagine you getting away with anything."

"I was sneaky." She's now got on the dress that screams sin and walks over and takes my hand, pulling me up off the bed and leading me to one of her windows. "See how this part of the roof is sort of flat? I'd sit out here and smoke sometimes. And then there's that tree there. See its strong branches?"

"You didn't?" I say because I can't picture Vale shimmying down that tree in the middle of the night.

"I was a bad girl," she says with a wicked grin.

The smile slides off my face as thoughts of her sneaking out to hook up with Trent invade my brain.

"But not that bad," she says, her eyes flashing shyly up to mine.

"So, you and Trent never—"

"No, we didn't. I wasn't dumb. I knew about contraceptives and all that, but I had big dreams, Carter, and it just wasn't worth the risk to me. No way in hell was I going to get knocked up and stuck with a baby and my high school boyfriend. Not that it's bad if people do. I know it happens a lot. I have friends it happened to, and they are still here, happily married. It's just not what I wanted for *me*."

A grin spreads across my face. I can't even help it.

She swats my shoulder. "Carter Crawford. I know what you are thinking."

"And what's that?" I ask, eyebrow raised in defiance.

"You are happy that I didn't sleep with Trent."

"Damn right I am. This whole time, he's been acting like ... well, like you two did sleep together. So, if nothing else, I can go to the club, feeling pretty pleased. Because you and me, Vale? Well, we most definitely have."

I expect her to say something sexy. Tell me how much she enjoyed our times together.

Instead, she says, "You were jealous."

In one quick motion, I wrap my arms around her and pin her against the window. "Jealous?"

"Mmhmm." She smirks.

"What do I have to be jealous about?"

"Your smile said it all, Carter," she says, but then the smirk slides off her face just as my mouth gravitates toward hers.

"I didn't think you would be jealous. I … well, I thought you hated me. After what you told me, you know, on the phone that day. But the kiss on the porch, it felt good. I mean, at least for me."

Her eyes are wide in question. Her face and lips turned up toward mine.

I should walk away. Tell her that she's right. That she means nothing to me. But I know that would be my wounded pride talking.

"I don't hate you, Vale. I never could. No matter what happened." I let go of her and turn around. If I hadn't, I would have just kissed her again. And I can't keep kissing her.

That's why I asked her if we could be friends when we got back to LA. Now is not the time to discuss our relationship. The what-ifs, the what-could-bes. We just need to get through this weekend, make her family happy for her, and then go home and talk about what really happened that night. At some point, I need to tell her. Just not here. Not now.

She stands by the window a little longer, just staring at me. I put on my watch, grab my wallet and phone, and shove them in my pocket.

"Now that you know the truth," she says, "can you be nice to Trent tonight?"

"I've been nice to Trent all day," I smart, trying to act like I don't care about their relationship.

Whether or not they had sex doesn't really matter—whatever they had certainly stuck with the poor guy. And honestly, I know what it feels like to be in love with her. And how it can hurt when she doesn't love you back. Trent and I might have to form a club.

She grits her teeth and looks down at the dresser. "I know. I'm sure it's not easy for him to see me engaged."

"I guess that means giving him a play-by-play of our sex life is out of the question?" I joke.

"Carter …" she pleads. And the look on her face is similar to the one she wore when she was down on her knees this morning.

"Hey, Carter? Waiting on you, buddy!" Blake calls out from downstairs.

And for once, I am grateful for the interruption.

"Have fun tonight," I tell her. When she frowns at me, I cave because I hate seeing her unhappy. "I promise to be nice to Trent, and I'll make sure AJ has fun but stays out of trouble."

She comes over, stands on her tiptoes, and kisses me on the lips. "Thank you."

And with the kiss comes clarity. Trent is still pining for her because they never slept together. He probably hoped that when she came home, they would. If for no other reason than to get her out of his system. And I wonder if that would work for me. But I know better than Trent. I know that you don't get over a girl like her.

She gives me a cocky grin. It's the same one I got the night we met after she beat me in a video game.

She leans her sexy-ass self closer to me and says, "Just so we're clear on this, Carter Crawford, my fiancé would have a fun night out with the guys. But then he would come home to me."

I practically growl with need. With only a few words, she can get me all worked up.

She takes a step back and studies me, knowing this is how I usually looked before we would have sex, because she goes, "If this were real between us, that's what I would expect."

"Oh," I say, trying to pull myself back together before going downstairs to meet my fake soon-to-be brother-in-law.

GLITTER CONFETTI BOMBS.

EVERYONE IS GATHERED on the porch, but no one really knows what I have planned. I wanted to surprise all of them, I guess. I hired a professional photographer to capture all our fun moments tonight, and I know this will be the first big photo op.

I hand a *Bride-to-Be* sash to Raine and the sparkly tiara veil to Brooke. "Can you put these on her? And smile for the camera."

They have fun, getting Lakelyn dressed up. Soon, everyone takes turns, posing with Lakelyn, both individually and in fun group shots in front of the massive pink balloon arch I had set up in the front yard.

And there might be hot-pink penis balloons sticking out between the pale balloons, and it really cracks me up that no one has noticed them yet. But they are too busy posing.

"Hey, Lakelyn," I call out. "Why don't we get a photo of you sucking on one of the balloons?"

She looks confused at first, and my sister is all like, "That's so dangerous."

Which is true for children, obviously, because the balloon could break and they could choke and die and that is no laughing matter, but when Lakelyn moves closer, she starts laughing and pinging the little penises with her finger, making them bounce up and down. Even though she hasn't hit the champagne yet, it causes her to laugh hysterically.

"Suck on it," her college roommate yells out, and before we know it, all the college girls are pretending to suck the balloons.

Of course, that's the exact moment when Grandma and Aunt Helen choose to come out on the front porch.

"Well, my word," Grandma says. "Doesn't that look like fun?" And next thing I know, she's over with the girls, bouncing around one of the hot-pink penis balloons then squeezing it and making comments like, "It's not quite firm enough yet," which causes Lakelyn and the girls—and, well, me too—to practically die with laughter.

Tears are running down my face as Grandma continues making jokes.

Helen is about to join in on the fun when my mom walks out of the house and goes, "Mother!"

"Um, how about we do something else fun?" I suggest. Don't need Mom having a coronary before the big day.

I hand out glittery confetti bombs to all those in attendance, giving Grandma something else to do with her hands.

"All right," I say, "we only have one shot to get this right."

I explain to them how to shoot off their pops, and then the photographer gets us all lined up.

"One, two, three, pull!"

Suddenly, glitter confetti fills the air around us, raining down on Lakelyn, and I can already tell by the look on her face that it's going to be one of my favorite pictures.

"Time for shots!" one of the college girls calls out.

"How about a toast instead?" I offer, and when I

say it, I can barely believe my eyes.

My father comes out of the house, dressed in a tuxedo and white gloves, pushing a gold bar cart filled with an ice bucket full of the champagne I bought along with my mother's crystal flutes.

Tears immediately fill my eyes, and I have to blink them away.

Everyone gets their glasses filled, and we go stand back under the balloon arch for more photos.

"I'd like to start the toasts, if I may," my father says from the porch, causing my mouth to literally drop open, "and then I'll let the bachelorette party commence."

Lakelyn nods her head and smiles at Dad.

He holds his glass in front of him and says, "Lakelyn, may your life be filled with many more pink confetti moments. Cheers."

Everyone is in tears, my sisters and me especially. I don't know how my dad did it. He's not the sentimental type, but he just managed to describe the perfect life for my bubbly, sparkling sister in one sentence. Lakelyn rushes over and gives Dad a hug.

We do more toasts and take more photos, and then the stretch limo I ordered comes barreling down the driveway. I glance at my watch and notice that he is a couple of minutes late. Which actually worked out okay.

"A pink limo?! Eek!" Lakelyn screeches in excitement.

We take more photos outside the limo.

Grandma and Helen put up a pretend fuss about not going in the limo, but I tell them I left them each a bachelorette gift bag inside the house and that there is champagne in them, which seems to placate them.

I'm at the end of the line to get into the limo when I realize my father is standing next to me.

"I've been thinking all week about what I might say in my toast, but I just wanted to thank you. The decor you chose for Lakelyn and the confetti shower ... well, it's because of that, that I knew what to say. Even though you haven't been around much, it's clear you and your sister are still close."

I nod. I can't really say much because I don't understand what is happening here. *Is my father actually being nice to me?*

Finally, I get out, "Yeah, we are. She's a sweetheart."

"I'm trusting you girls to keep her outta trouble," my father says.

"I will," I agree.

Then, he grins and hands me an envelope full of cash. "And buy a couple of rounds on me."

My immediate thought is to hand it back to him because I don't need his money to buy shots to give my sister a fun bachelorette party, but I decide not to. Because I know he's doing this for her, not me.

"Thanks, Dad," I say. "I will."

INSIDE THE LIMO are gift bags for each girl with their names on them. They quickly find their bags and sit in the seat they were on. They squeal with delight over the little gifts inside. There are plastic champagne flutes, T-shirts marking the event, and necklaces I actually commissioned the jewelry designer Chloe Crawford—Carter's little sister—to make the second Lakelyn asked me to be her maid of honor. Fortunately, I have attended numerous events like this over my years—always the bridesmaid and never the bride and all that—and always stuck my favorite ideas away in the back of my brain, waiting for this occasion. Also inside are funny buttons for each girl to wear that will spark conversations at the bars we are going to. Things like: *Bad Influence, Trophy Wife, Cougar, Sassy Pants, Designated Drunk, Wild Thing, High Maintenance, Shameless, Gold Digger*, and of course, *Bride*.

"More champagne?" I ask, opening up the cooler in the limo and pulling out a couple of bottles of Cristal. I didn't use it for the toast at the house, figuring my father would have a fit over it, but what Daddy doesn't know won't hurt him, *right*?

"Is that Cristal?" Raine exclaims. "I've always wanted to try that kind, but it's pretty pricey."

"Not something I drink every day," I tell them, although, actually, I sort of do. My new bungalow in LA doesn't have much in the fridge, but it is stocked with a case of this. I don't splurge on much, but …

whatever.

The girls all cheer as I pop the cork on two bottles and pass them around.

We're almost into town when one of the girls finally asks, "So, where are we going?"

"It's going to be sort of a pub crawl. A different bar every half hour. And I have some fun tasks for you. As if showing up in a pink limo full of women isn't enough."

I reach in my bag and grab a glittery pink velvet sign to go around Lakelyn's neck that says, *Kiss the Miss Good-Bye.*

"Ah, this is so cute!" But then she stares at it. "I don't get it."

I hand her the matching pink velvet string-closure purse. "Guys have to pay you a dollar, which they put in the purse, and then they get to kiss you on the cheek."

"I bet some of them will want to kiss her on the lips." One of her college friends screech-laughs.

"Oh, I don't want to kiss anyone else," Lakelyn says, looking concerned.

"And you don't have to," I tell her. Then, I hand her a stack of cards. "Read these and give them to who you think they fit."

She reads a few, "*Dance on the bar.* Oh! That's for you, Rachel," she says to one of her college friends. She continues through the stack, handing out the fun cards I made with tasks like: *Use a cheesy pick-up line, Find a guy with the same first name as the groom, Get a guy to give you his tie—or another article of clothing, Get either wedding advice or a phone number written on a bar napkin, Take a picture with a hottie, Photobomb a stranger, Get a piggyback ride, Kiss the bartender*, and other fun things to keep the party going.

The limo stops at our first location, which is more of a sports bar hangout place than the type of club we'll end the night with.

With the tight party dresses we're wearing, the glow-in-the-dark penis necklaces most of the girls have on, as well as the bachelorette party temporary tattoos from the gift bags, let's just say, we definitely turn a few heads away from the sports on TV.

Along with the fun name tags and challenges, we've bought a lot of shots, and guys literally line up with their dollar bills to give Lakelyn a kiss on the cheek.

CHAPTER TWELVE
MISTER GOOD TIME.

Carter

"Gentlemen, we have arrived." Blake's already on his third shot by the time we pull up in front of the club.

As we get out of the limo, I notice Trent looks a little sweaty. "You all right?" I ask him.

"I'm not feeling great. Probably should've taken it easier today." He flashes a brief smile. "Thanks for asking."

"Come on, BTO. It's my bachelor party!" AJ flings an arm around Trent's neck and drags him into the club.

I bring up the rear.

The second we're in the VIP section, Blake says to our waitress, "We'll start with shots. A round of Alabama Slammers!"

"As long as we don't end up in the slammer tonight!" Trent yells out.

"Wouldn't be the first time for you, Blake," Jake says. "How many times has your daddy had to bail your drunk ass out in the morning?"

"Like, twice," Blake says.

"And me?" Jake counters.

"Like, once," Blake says.

"And what about me?" Seth says, laughing and slapping Blake on the back.

And I can't help but enjoy their camaraderie. It reminds me of how my brothers and I tease each other.

"Okay, fine," Blake says, "I might like to whoop it up on occasion. It's all in good fun."

"Yeah, drunk fighting always is," AJ jokes, but he looks at me and rolls his eyes.

As *BTO* and Blake high-five, I realize drinking isn't the only thing I need to worry about.

"Speaking of good fun," Blake says, sliding his hand on the waitress's ass like he knows her on a personal level, "Shauna here has our shots!" He holds up a glass and says, "To the groom! AJ, buddy, we're getting you drunk tonight!"

AJ leans over and clinks his shot glass with mine. "Don't worry. I work too hard on my body." He lowers his voice and says, "I follow Danny Diamond's D3 regimen. I'll have a beer every now and then, but nights like these, I drink a glass of water between every drink."

"That's smart," I tell him.

Because if the strip club were more like a show, it would have been fine. But when you combine lap dances with alcohol, I've seen things get stupid—fast.

Fortunately, I don't represent the kind of athletes who need to be babysat on a regular basis.

Blake is calling for more shots.

The group is getting tipsy.

Our VIP section is full of dancers.

"Which one's the groom?" one of them asks with a wide smile.

I pat AJ on the shoulder before two dancers take him, one on either arm, and sit him down in the booth. Blake is chatting up another pair of dancers and instructing them to keep AJ happy all night while someone else orders more shots.

"Carter Crawford?" A familiar face appears in the crowd just beyond our roped-off area. "Dude! Did you sign AJ?"

"Billy Summers," I say, shaking his hand and being cordial.

But his showing up does not thrill me. He's an extremely talented cornerback with a reputation for the kind of wild nights that are starting to affect his career.

"And, no, he's not my client."

"Then, why are you here?"

"It's his bachelor party. I'm attending the wedding with the future bride's sister."

"No shit." Billy turns to our group and says, "AJ, buddy. Congrats. Next round is on me!"

Cheers erupt as they all greet Billy and discuss

how his latest pro team, Cleveland, might do next season.

Billy quickly works his way back to me. "So, Carter Crawford, I don't know if you've heard, but I'm looking for a new agent."

"I didn't know you and Paul had parted ways."

"Yeah, I got tired of his bitching at me. You interested?"

"I'm afraid my stable is full right now." No way I have the time or energy to babysit someone like him.

"Oh, dog," he says, "I just realized. AJ's sister. You're talking Vale Martin. The smoking-hot supermodel. I remember now that you were dating." Billy grins at me, quickly moving on. "Isn't this place great? Best strip club in a hundred miles. I'm from a small town about twenty miles over. My dad buys farm equipment from the Martins." He glances away from me, looking at AJ, who is standing a little awkwardly as women dance around him.

The club is packed. And with Blake's big mouth, and he and Trent's love for fighting—mixed with alcohol-fueled testosterone and guys wanting to prove themselves—the night probably won't end well.

Billy, whose presence only adds to the volatility of the situation, says to me, "Gotta get that boy a lap dance. Maybe send him back to the private room, if ya know what I mean. I'm gonna go grab my friends. We can all celebrate together. We'll keep the groom busy with the ladies, so we can talk about why you need to represent the great Billy Summers."

I look around.

The drinks are flowing.

Everyone seems to be having fun.

Everyone, except for AJ, who is sipping water and trying to avoid getting another lap dance, and Trent, who is sitting on one of the velvet couches, running a hand across his forehead.

I go over and hand him a bottle of water. "You don't look so good. Maybe I should call you a car, take you home."

"Nah, I'm fine," he says, but the way he's grimacing tells another story.

"Are you sure? You're sweating. Are you feeling sick?"

"Yeah, maybe. Probably something I ate. But I'm supposed to be here for AJ." He jerks his chin in the groom's direction.

"He's doing okay. And I'll keep an eye on him." I take a seat next to Trent and pat his shoulder. "You can sit this out. He needs you to be there for him on Saturday after all."

Trent gives me a glance that's anything but friendly. "So, that's how it is, huh? You step in and act like you own the place. Just like how you tried to shove money at me earlier. Now, a friend of yours *happens* to be here, and he's buying drinks. You're Mr. Good Time, aren't you?"

Only the fact that I promised Vale I would be nice to him keeps me from chewing him out. "I'm sorry if that's how you took my wanting to chip in, pull my weight. And I thought we were *all* here to have a good time."

"Yeah, well, you're pretty good at being where you don't belong. Like with Vale."

And I can't help it. Vale is not his. Not that she's technically mine either, but at least I've slept with her. Many times. So, screw him and his unrequited love. Forget about Mr. Good Time. I'm done being Mr. Nice Guy. Trent needs to be put in his place.

"It's my understanding that you and Vale have not spoken even once since she left town. She's my fiancée, and what you are insinuating and the way you look at her is wildly inappropriate. It needs to stop."

Trent presses a hand to his side, and I'm getting concerned about the guy. When he winces enough to bare his clenched teeth, I wave AJ over.

"I guess you figured out the secret," Trent grunts out.

"What secret?"

"To getting Vale to agree to marry you. She said no when I asked her."

The room goes silent around me, or maybe it's all in my head. "You asked her to marry you?"

"The night before she left town, yeah. I was hoping it would be enough to get her to stay. It wasn't."

He leans back against the sofa, closing his eyes. "Oh hell, I'm in bad shape."

"I'm calling an ambulance," I tell AJ, who sits down next to Trent.

"Dude, you don't look so good," AJ says, who, along with Seth, helps us get him outside for some fresh air.

"He shouldn't have come," I tell AJ as red flashing lights approach the club. "He wasn't feeling well earlier."

The paramedic assesses Trent and announces they are taking him to the hospital.

"Should I go with him?" AJ asks.

"No, you stay here and enjoy your party. I'll go with him," Seth offers.

ONCE EVERYONE IN the group hears about Trent, the party seems to lose steam, and thankfully, before long, we're back in the limo, heading home.

I'm pissed Vale didn't tell me that Trent had proposed. And I hate that she acted naive about why he'd been hanging around for years.

I also can't help but feel a little bad for Trent.

WE'LL FINISH THIS LATER.

Vale

"OHMIGAWD, THIS WAS the best night ever!" Lakelyn throws back her head and howls at the moon on our way to the limo. I mean, she literally howls at the moon.

Her tiara is askew, but she looks happy and tipsy and is having a ball.

"Careful. We don't want you twisting an ankle before your wedding," I say, trying to make sure she gets safely to the limo. I'm a little tipsy myself, but at least I'm not wearing five-inch stilettos like she is. Nights like these, I prefer a platform wedge, as they are easier to walk in.

She skips the entire way to the limo, ignoring my warnings and giggling. "Tonight was so much fun. All the bars. The scavenger hunt. And this last club was the best! It's exactly what I wanted. Letting loose and dancing with my girls!"

That causes all the girls to chant and cheer with her.

"You're the best!" she says, wrapping an arm around me. "I'm so glad you're here."

Once everyone gets loaded into the limo, she turns to me and says, "I love you so much."

"I love you too."

"No. I mean, I *really* love you." She takes my hands and stares into my eyes. "Seriously. I'm not just saying this because I'm drunk. I love you. Having you here has meant the world to me, and we're not even at the wedding yet."

"I'm so happy to be here for you."

"And tonight was super perfect."

"You're buzzed off the drinks, the music, and the guys. They were flocking to you!"

"It was fun, but there was only one man I was thinking about tonight. I miss AJ."

The girls in the limo make a collective sigh, and Lakelyn says, "You know what would finish the night off perfectly?"

"Stopping at a drive-through for some burgers and fries?" I ask her. "It's our next stop."

"You think of everything!"

TWENTY MINUTES LATER, we're all chowing down on burgers, fries, and milkshakes.

"Good thinking, Vale," Raine says with a mouthful of food. "We needed something to soak up all that pink shit we were drinking. What was that?"

"I don't know, but it was good," Lakelyn says with a laugh. "And it was pink, so it totally fit."

"That's because of me," Brooke says. "One of my challenges was to get the bartender to create a special drink for the bride."

"It was very yummy," Raine says. "And very, very

strong."

"I wonder how the guys are doing," Brooke says as she dips a fry into her chocolate shake.

"Ew. How can you eat that?" Lakelyn asks.

"You've never dipped a fry?"

"No! That's gross!"

"I'm with Brooke on this." I shrug. So does Raine. "You should try it."

"No, thank you."

"Have you ever had a chocolate-covered potato chip?"

"Yeah, but the chocolate isn't icy cold at the time."

I roll my eyes while dipping a fry. "Try it," I insist as I hold it out to her. "I can't believe we never taught you this, growing up."

She takes it, looks at it like it might bite, and then shoves it into her mouth all at once.

"You'd think I'd asked her to eat a bug," I mutter, which causes all the college girls to snicker.

They are already dipping fries and loving it.

"Ohmigawd, how did I not know about this?" Lakelyn pulls the lid off her shake and dunks a handful of fries in at once. "This is revolutionary. We could market this, you guys."

"We clearly failed as big sisters." Raine laughs.

Brooke holds up a hand. "Well, I know the guys aren't having this much fun, no matter what Blake had planned."

"He's trouble," Lakelyn mumbles. At least, that's what I think she said with all those fries in there.

"His heart's in the right place," I insist.

"You've always had a soft spot for him, just like Mom and Dad." Raine snorts.

"I wouldn't go that far. At least I can admit he gets himself into lots more trouble than they've ever been aware of. I don't know how he does it."

"If he ever decides on a life of crime, he's gonna be very good at it." Lakelyn goes for more fries, dunking them into her shake. She might be a little tipsier than I thought.

I tried to drink the perfect amount tonight. Just wanted a little buzz. But then I downed a couple of good-bye shots as we were leaving the club, and I should have known better than that. I really don't drink all that much. Usually just sip on champagne when I'm at a party or an event. I honestly don't remember the last time I did shots.

Shit. Actually, I do. It was a night filled with Carter, Mexican food, tequila shooters, and more Carter. We were both a little drunk, and let's just say, I am very glad I didn't drink so much that I don't remember everything.

In fact, it's making me feel horny, just thinking about it.

Between that and the kiss session on the front porch, he's most definitely on my mind.

WE GET DROPPED off at the house, and as I climb the stairs, I remember that I'm sharing a room with Carter. And if I have anything to say about it, we'll be sharing my bed too.

It doesn't matter that we aren't together. We used to have sex with no strings all the time. No commitments. There's no reason we can't do that tonight.

Only he isn't in the room when I get here. The bed is still made. His cologne has faded to almost nothing.

I poke my head into the hallway. "The boys aren't back yet?"

Lakelyn snickers, giggling her way toward me. "Guess not. Maybe they stopped off for burgers too. Ooh, do you think AJ would bring me more fries?" She pats her stomach. "Oh, what am I thinking? I can't eat like that and fit into my dress." She gives me another hug and says, "I need sleep now."

WHILE I'M WAITING for Carter to get home, I change into the tank top and boy shorts I brought as pajamas. Not the sexiest thing I own, but when I packed, seducing him was the last thing on my mind. I was feeling so nervous about coming back home that the thought never crossed my mind.

But those thoughts came rushing back the second I stepped in Carter's house and went into his room, into his closet.

I fall back on the bed, thinking about how we met. I was at a Super Bowl pre-party, surrounded by pretty people—professional athletes, sportscasters, celebrities. We were pitted against each other in a video game contest. Had a blast. I'm still not sure if he let me win. Either way, we had chemistry. I invited him back to my hotel room. It was hot. We had more than sparks, yet we started out as friends. We were good together. It's a fun thing—when you like someone's company as much as you like sex with them.

I sprawl myself across the bed in what I know is both a sexy and very flattering pose.

The door opens, and Carter comes in with a sigh. "What a night," he groans, running his hands through his hair.

But he stops for a beat and takes a long look at me.

I'm ready for him to pounce as I purr, "Same here. Did you guys have fun?"

"Some of us did, yeah." He takes his shoes off, starting to undress, and it gets me even more hot and bothered.

"So did we. And I was just lying here, thinking back to all the fun we used to have. Nights tangled up in your sheets."

"Oh, really?"

"Oh, yeah."

"So, you were grinding on guys at the club and

thinking of me?" he asks, looking over his shoulder at me.

"I suppose I was." I slide one bare leg against the other. I know my boobs are spilling out of my tank.

And I know he won't be able to resist. He's going to leap onto this bed and do exactly what I've been dreaming about.

Instead, he sighs, turning his back to me, and unbuttons his shirt. "If it's any consolation, none of the strippers were as pretty as you."

Oh, this is promising.

"So, you were thinking along those lines too?"

"I couldn't help it either."

My breath hitches when I get a look at his broad, muscled back. Those shoulders. Those arms. How many nights did I hold on to them tightly as we …

But then he turns to me, unbuttoning his jeans. "I had a lot of other things on my mind though too."

Oh jeez, does he want to talk? I don't want to talk.

I just want to borrow that thing I know is hiding under his boxers. Maybe I should just spread my legs apart and not say a word. Give him an open invitation.

This thought causes me to giggle to myself. *Okay, so I might be slightly more than tipsy.*

He keeps going. "AJ had fun but stayed out of trouble." He takes off his pants, leaving him in nothing but tight boxer briefs.

I'm practically panting by the time he gets into

bed.

I snuggle up to him and glide a finger across his bicep, up to his shoulder, and then over his chest. "I've missed this. Being with you like this."

"Have you?"

"I've spent half the night thinking about us. And I wondered when you were going to do what you said out on the porch. You know, we'll finish this later."

He covers my hand with his, bringing it to a stop before I can trail it down his abdomen.

"You know what I spent half the night thinking about?"

"What?" I purr, straining upward, hoping for a kiss.

"The fact that you never told me Trent proposed the night before you left town."

PAST THAT POINT.

Carter

I CAN TELL she is tipsy and horny. If I were a smart man, I would go for it.

But I didn't sign up for all this shit, and I'm pissed.

She bolts upright. "What?"

"You heard me. He proposed. You ran off. And you have the audacity to act like you don't know why he's been waiting for you all these years, hoping you'll change your mind. Did you even bother turning him down, or did you leave him hanging on purpose, so you'd have a fallback plan?"

"How dare you," she says.

"How dare I bring up something you should've told me before you dragged me into this situation? No wonder it's been so awkward around him. He wasn't just your boyfriend. He wanted to *marry* you."

Her mouth opens and then snaps shut.

"So, I'm sorry if I didn't fall in line with this seduction scene or whatever you had in mind, but I'm not in the mood to get the runaround all over again. At least I know I'm not the only man in your life who did. Maybe good old BTO and I should start a club."

"Screw you." She turns her back on me, flopping back down on the bed.

"I'd say we're past that point." I stare down at her hair and try to tell myself to keep it in my pants. Even though I care about what Trent told me, my dick couldn't care less. "Oh, and by the way, I did what you asked and was nice to Trent tonight. Got to know him better. Even called an ambulance for him when he needed it."

"An ambulance?!" she says, turning back to face me. "Carter! Did you hurt him?"

I roll my eyes at her. "I just told you, I was nice to him."

"Then, why did he need an ambulance, and why are you just now telling me?"

"Sorry, I was too busy dealing with your boobs staring at me."

She lets out a sigh. "Carter, what happened? Did he get in a fight?"

"No. He wasn't feeling well earlier, said it was something he ate, but he was sweating and had abdominal pain. I called an ambulance, and Seth went with him to the hospital."

"Oh, poor Trent. I guess that put a damper on the night, huh?"

"Your brother did his best to keep the party going."

"I hope he's okay by the wedding."

"Wouldn't want to miss the chance to walk down the aisle next to him, huh?" I blurt out, feeling hurt.

Her face crumples. "I don't even want to be here," she says, getting emotional and rolling away from me.

But it doesn't seem to bother her for too long because she's asleep quickly while I lie next to her, staring at the ceiling and thinking.

Since New Year's Eve, I've wanted to call her and yell at her. Tell her what I saw. What I had planned.

I want her to know what she lost that night. But then I picture that guy's hands on her ass and know I did the right thing.

Especially after tonight. *Did she really think all it would take was draping herself over the bed, showing plenty of skin, and I'd fall right back into the same pattern as before? The pattern where I was basically her booty call?*

Even worse is the fact that I haven't slept with anyone since her.

CHAPTER THIRTEEN
SAVED HIS LIFE.

Vale

"YOU HAVE GOT to be kidding me." I pry one eye open and immediately slam it shut.

The sun's up, shining brightly through the window.

Why didn't I pull the shades last night?

Probably because I was more worried about getting laid.

Carter, however, seems pretty chipper. "Nothing like the sunrise to wake you."

"Morning comes early on the farm," I mumble before pulling the pillow over my head. "Even the morning after a big party."

"Good luck sleeping in," he says with a laugh.

I feel the bed move and know he's gotten up. Moments later, I hear the shower turn on in the bathroom. And he's right. There are already sounds coming from the kitchen downstairs. Mom has probably been up, cooking for a while.

I wish I could stay in bed all day. To hide from

Carter more than anything.

I should have told him more about Trent.

Prepared him.

But it's been years, and even I didn't know what to expect.

I just knew that Trent would be the best man. That he and AJ were still close.

And that he was still single.

Carter doesn't waste any time in getting ready. It feels like moments later, and he's coming out of the bathroom, dressed, freshly shaven, and looking incredibly handsome.

"Come on, Vale. Time to rise and shine. Lots of family fun planned for today. And I just can't wait." He says all of this in a mock happy tone.

He's mad at me. And I need to make things right.

"Just for the record, Carter, I was a little tipsy last night, but I wasn't drunk." What I should have done was kept my mouth shut, waited until he got into bed, and then kissed him. I know that's all it would have taken. "I'm sorry if I acted, you know, inappropriately."

Carter chuckles and then licks his lips, and somehow, I know exactly what he is thinking—about just how many *inappropriate* things he used to do to me.

Well, not inappropriate—unless you're sleeping down the hall from your parents.

"Last night was rough," he says, running his hand through his hair in frustration. "Everyone was trying to get AJ as drunk as possible. I had to be the responsible one for people I barely knew. Trent was hurting. He told me that he proposed. Then, I came back to find you …" He waves his hand through the air. "Let's just try to get through the next couple of days and pretend like we like each other."

"Love," I say.

"What?" His eyes go wide.

"We're supposed to *love* each other."

His shoulders slump down, and he lets out a sigh. "That's not hard to pretend, Vale. I did love you."

"But then … why?" I ask.

He shakes his head.

I hop out of bed, irritated again. "Plus, you haven't signed AJ yet."

He rolls his eyes at me before opening the bedroom door. "I did this for you, Vale. And no other reason."

After he walks out the door, I plop back down on the bed. Because … *he loved me?*

THE SHOWER PERKS me up, but I'm still reeling from Carter's statement. And I'm confused as hell. *He loved me. But then told me that I wasn't the girl for him?*

I braid my wet hair, get dressed, and then pad

barefoot downstairs, following the aroma of bacon and, if memory serves me right, chocolate chip pancakes. Lakelyn's favorite.

When I make my way into the kitchen, I'm surprised to discover that I'm one of the last people to arrive. And it's barely eight o'clock. I'm fine with getting up for early call times, but after rolling in at two this morning, I didn't expect this.

"Mmm, pancakes." I help myself to a couple stacked on a platter before adding some bacon. *When on the farm.* "Pancakes happen to be one of Carter's specialties," I blurt out before I think better of it.

He shoots me a look from his seat at the table.

Mom turns from the stove. "I wish I had known. I could've used some help."

"Next time," he promises my mom as he shoots daggers at me.

Carter always made me pancakes for breakfast. And one time, when his younger brother, Cash, was over with his now-wife Ashlyn, they told me that he only made them for girls he really liked. It made me feel giddy, knowing he did that for me.

He loved me?

Why didn't he tell me?

Although I suppose I should ask myself the same question. I never told him how I felt either.

Raine comes in through the kitchen door, followed by Seth. They're each carrying a child on their hip.

"Hey, how's Trent?" Carter asks.

Seth winces. "It was his appendix. He had surgery to remove it."

"Oh no!" Mom gasps, a hand to her chest.

"He's lucky actually. Thank goodness for Carter," Seth says.

"Why thank goodness for Carter?" I ask.

"Because if he hadn't paid attention to how much BTO was hurting and called an ambulance— heck, we were all drinking too much. None of the rest of us noticed. The doctors say it was close to rupturing, and that would have been life-threatening."

"Is he doing okay now?" my mother asks. "Did you stay with him?"

"No, I rode to the hospital with him and then called his mom. She came to the hospital and texted me early this morning. I would have updated you all, but I didn't want to wake anyone."

Lakelyn hugs Carter from behind. "You're practically a hero."

Carter tries to wave it off, but I can see the slight flush on his cheeks. "It was nothing."

"No, it wasn't," Seth insists, patting his shoulder on the way to the feast spread out across the island. "He's a stubborn son of a bitch."

"Language, please," Mom murmurs, sliding fresh pancakes onto the platter.

"I'm just saying, he was determined to stick it out

last night and be a good best man. If *I* had called an ambulance, he would've knocked me flat on my … backside." He glances at Mom, who gives him an approving smile.

"I doubt he had it in him to knock anyone on their backside last night," Carter says, looking thoughtful as he eats a piece of bacon.

"Thank you regardless, Carter." Mom pours him some fresh coffee and kisses his cheek before moving on to the next cup.

The gesture pulls at my heart. Because Carter fits here.

With my family. With me.

And I have to remind myself that it's not real.

"I HEAR WE'RE down a best man," my father announces, walking into the room and pouring what's probably his third cup of the day.

I've never seen anyone drink as much coffee as he does.

When AJ follows behind him, I can only assume they've been discussing the situation.

"Trent will be okay," I offer.

"I know. It's just a shame this had to happen now," AJ says. "I'm sure he'll feel bad about missing the wedding."

He takes a plate, filling it with food, and then sits down next to Lakelyn. Lakelyn finishes eating and then pulls the pink purse from last night up from her lap and onto the table, where she starts taking out and then counting dollar bills.

"Dollars?" AJ says with a laugh. "Were those supposed to be for the male strippers last night?"

"If you must know," Lakelyn says, her eyebrows raised in delight and a goofy smile on her face, "while you were out spending all your dollars last night, I was out, making them."

AJ's eyes go wide, and it's obvious he's trying to imagine his future bride pole dancing. Finally, he just looks confused. "How did you make them?"

"Guys lined up in the bars we were at to kiss her," I offer with a smirk.

"Yeah," Lakelyn says, pulling out the little badge she wore.

"*Kiss the Miss Good-Bye?*" AJ says, reading it. "Wait. You kissed guys last night?"

"What's good for the goose is good for the gander," my father offers with a chuckle. "You were at a strip club last night."

AJ ignores him, asking Lakelyn, "How many guys did you kiss?"

She holds up a finger at him and continues counting her money. "Forty-two. And they kissed me." AJ's jaw tightens before Lakelyn says, "Only on the cheek."

AJ lets out a sigh of relief, and everyone else starts laughing.

THE RIGHT FIT.

Carter

I'M STANDING OUT on the front porch with AJ. There isn't a lot that shocks me, but this does.

"You want me to step in?" I say unbelievably.

Why would he ask me when he has Blake? Seth? Jake?

Literally anyone else?

AJ chuckles. "Yeah, man. I would love it if you did."

"I'm honored you would ask. Don't get me wrong."

He jams his hands into his pockets. "You did a great job last night. You looked after me. You really stepped up, even before Trent left. You feel like the right guy, and my instincts are never wrong." He chuckles. "And Lakelyn thinks it's perfect, with Vale being the MOH."

"What's MOH?"

"*Maid Of Honor.* You'd better learn the lingo if you're gonna do this. Though seriously, I'm asking mostly because you're the right fit."

The right fit. I can't help but think how we're the right fit in a professional sense. He's a good kid.

Lots of thoughts are running through my head. One being how I will be in the photos that this family will cherish for the rest of their lives. Another about how I pride myself on being an honest person but that I'm lying to everyone here. I glance at Vale, wondering how I got myself into this mess but knowing it's because I couldn't say no to her. That I wouldn't say no to spending time with her even if it meant lying to the world.

I realize that I'm still hurt over what happened—or didn't happen—between us. Because even though my true thoughts occasionally sneak out of my mouth, for the most part, I'm kind of acting like a little bitch to her. Trying to make her pay for kissing another guy instead of what I should be doing—trying to win her back.

Wait. Win her back?

No.

No. No. No.

Definitely don't want her back. At least, not the way things were before.

My sister was right. Sex is not the way to a girl's heart, and neither is apathy.

AJ continues, "Just stand up there next to me. Make sure I have the ring. Maybe keep an eye on me if I have a little too much to drink tonight at the rehearsal dinner—you've seen how Blake tries to make sure everyone's keeping up with him."

"Yes, I have." And I played interference for much of last night.

"It would mean a lot. Besides, you're practically

part of the family now. Might as well jump in, right?"

I force a smile. *Yes. Part of the family.*

"Sure. I'd be honored, truly."

We shake hands to seal the deal before he goes back into the house.

Which is good because I need a minute.

Who would've thought I'd not only be a fake fiancé this weekend, but now a best man too?

Vale joins me on the porch and stands next to me at the railing overlooking lush rose bushes. "He asked you to fill in as best man?"

"How did you know?"

"I had a feeling. You did come through for him in a big way last night. You kept the night on track when Trent's appendix could've ruined everything." She nudges me a little. "And don't pretend you don't like it just a little bit. Taking his place. You've been here for less than twenty-four hours, and you're the hero of the family."

"I don't like it."

"Come on. Just a little?" She holds her thumb and forefinger maybe an inch apart.

"No, Vale, I don't. It's nice to be appreciated, but I hate lying to your family. I really, truly hate it. But I'm doing it for you."

"Well, if we're being truthful, I'm not sorry about trying to seduce you last night."

"Truce?" I ask because I don't want to fight with

her anymore or push her away. Or talk about last night.

"Let's blame it on the alcohol," she says. "Although it's too bad you weren't drunk too. Remember that night we did the tequila—"

"You told me you were only a little tipsy."

"Whatever. I don't want to fight with you. We can't. We're both fish out of water here."

"You aren't."

"You sure about that? I could barely eat my breakfast once my father entered the room."

"He does have an imposing presence," I agree.

"You're putting it mildly."

"Okay, so we're friends." I jerk my chin in the direction of the wide green lawn, where hay bales are being put to use as goal markers. "You'll be cheering me on out there while we're playing?"

"I sure will. I want to see you wipe the grass with them."

"They're your family and longtime friends."

"Even better." She winks. "They still think you're just a city slicker. I think they might need to be taught a lesson."

As she strolls away, she adds over her shoulder, "Just don't be surprised when I reward you with a great, big kiss for making me so proud."

And that alone makes me want to win.

CHAPTER FOURTEEN
A LITTLE COOLING OFF.

Vale

"WHEW!" BROOKE SAYS to me as Carter takes off his shirt.

"Hush!" I stop short of clamping a hand over her mouth.

"I just want to know why he didn't take his shirt off the second he got here. I would've had a completely different opinion of him," she says, fanning her face.

"You're terrible," I say with a laugh.

"Sorry," she says, but she really doesn't look sorry as she hands me a glass of iced tea from the picnic table.

Not that she's wrong. AJ and Carter have been dominating the wedding games all day long—from hay-baling to cornhole to wood chopping and now football. He's going to walk out of this weekend a living legend by the time all is said and done.

The men are well into their flag football game— the last big event of the day. It's like a carnival out here with everyone laughing and cheering and trash-talking. All in good fun, of course.

At least, I think it is.

"Come on, AJ! Show that city boy what you're made of, son!"

I have to turn my head and roll my eyes at my father's outburst. Clearly, there's only one city boy on the field. Carter is the quarterback, and his team is just short of the goal. The score is 24 to 20, in favor of AJ's side.

I can't believe I'm so invested in this silly game, but I am. If for no other reason than to prove some kind of point to my father.

"Come on, Carter!" I shout, jumping up and down with my arms over my head. "You can do it, baby!"

I'm shocked when he turns and winks at me before taking his stance. And I about melt into a little puddle.

AJ is directly across from him.

"AJ will go for the sack," Lakelyn predicts.

"He's very fast for a man of his size," I admit. Really, he's going to kill it in the pros, no matter where he signs. "But Carter will get it away before he has the chance. Wait and see."

"You feel like putting money on it?"

"You got it. Ten bucks."

We pinkie-swear as Carter makes his calls and then takes the snap.

AJ bursts into motion, rolling through the offensive line.

"There you go!" Lakelyn squeals.

But her joy is premature because Carter fakes right and then goes left, spinning away from AJ. He cuts up the middle and practically walks into the end zone.

"Yes! That's what I'm talking about!" Not only am I excited to beat the team my dad was cheering for, but I also can't help but sit here and drool over Carter.

My fake fiancé is damn fine.

And he kicked ass in all the events. Even hay-baling, which he had never done before today, seemed to come naturally to him. I know better than anyone here how he takes care of his body, and even I was impressed.

"My champion." I take Carter's face between my hands, plant a big smacker of a kiss on his lips, and then throw my arms around his neck.

"Oh my gosh, get me out of here," he whispers in my ear as he hugs me. "I feel like I need to curl up in the fetal position and sleep for three days."

"So, there's being in shape, and there's killing oneself to look good in front of strangers. I see. I know just what to do." I take him by the hand and lead him to the shed, where we used to keep all the bicycles. Sure enough, they're still there, and it looks like they've been used recently.

"What are we doing?" Carter asks. "Don't tell me there are bike races next."

"Games are over. I was thinking you might be in the mood for a swim." I straddle my bike and tuck my long, flowing skirt around my legs before settling in on the seat. "I know I could use a little cooling off."

"You sure we shouldn't hang around?"

"So you can be adored and congratulated?" I stick my tongue out at him and take off, leaving him scrambling to catch up.

I loved riding bikes as a kid. Still do. It feels so freeing. My hair blowing back in the breeze. I could ride around here all day. But I have somewhere special I want to take Carter. Someplace I can't wait to show him.

Carter falls in beside me. "You know something?"

"What?"

"I don't think I've ever seen you look this happy."

Am I happy right now?

Strangely enough, yes, I am. The last thing I expected was to feel happy during my first visit home in so long, but then again, I didn't expect to be here with Carter.

YOUR TIMING SUCKS.

Carter

"SO, THIS IS a swimming hole." I prop the bike up with the kickstand, next to Vale's.

"Mmhmm." She's already sliding out of her sandals.

"Are you serious?"

"About what?" she asks as she unbuttons her blouse.

"About taking all your clothes off and jumping into the water."

"We did it as kids all the time. I'm only stripping down to my undies," she assures me as she keeps unbuttoning. "What, are you chicken?"

"Chicken?" I jerk a thumb toward where we just came from. "After what I did today? It's been a long time since I've had a man of AJ's size barreling toward me."

She throws her head back and laughs, and what a sound it is. I wasn't kidding when I said I'd never seen her look so happy.

"For what it's worth, you looked cool as a cucumber." Before I can thank her for that, she slides out of her skirt, leaving herself wearing nothing but skimpy white panties and a matching bra.

Fuck. She's a vision. The things I could do to her

right now. Even with most of the muscles in my body already aching, my manhood is still feeling … well, *cocky*.

Vale turns and grabs for a knotted length of rope slung over a thick limb. After a few experimental tugs, she grasps one of the upper knots, steps back, and then breaks into a run.

All I can do is hold my breath as she swings out over the water. She lets go with a shriek and plummets down, making a big splash.

Seconds later, she pops up, laughing. "It feels great! Get in here!"

What am I supposed to say to that? I strip down to my underwear and pray the rope will hold me. It looks like it's been out here for a long time.

Only one way to find out. I test it with a few tugs, and then I run and swing the way she did.

One big splash, and I'm shocked by how chilly the water is, but I do agree. It feels great.

"See?" she asks when I surface. "Just what we needed. So refreshing after being in the sun all day."

"You? You needed refreshed?"

Her laughter rings out in the tree-lined space. Really, we might as well be in our own little world out here. The sense of privacy doesn't do anything but inflame my desire.

We did say we were going to be friends from here on out, right? What could be more friendly than a quickie in the lake?

She takes a few strokes away from me, almost like she senses the struggle and figures it's better to give me some space. "It's been years since I've been out here. Not since …"

The way she stops catches my attention. "Since when?"

"It doesn't matter."

"You sure about that?"

She shakes her head, her arms moving back and forth in front of her as she treads water. "I shouldn't have brought it up. I wasn't thinking. But … I came out here the night before I left home."

Oh.

"In case you were wondering," she adds, "it wasn't a proper proposal. There was no ring. No getting down on one knee. It was spur of the moment. A desperate last-ditch effort to keep me here." She throws herself back until she's floating faceup, eyes closed. "I couldn't accept. Not like that. Not when it was desperation that had made him ask."

"What was so wrong with him wanting to keep you around?"

She hits me with a look out of the corner of her eye. "We were kids, Carter. We had no business getting married at that age. At least, I know I didn't. I knew myself well enough to know that it wouldn't work out. And he wasn't the kind of man I dreamed about, even back then." She pulls herself upright with a sigh. "It's not easy, knowing yourself at such a young age. No one believes you when you say you know what's best for you."

For the first time, I can see things through her eyes. Not that I've ever blamed her for leaving home and striking out on her own. I admire that and still do.

Again, it's like she can sense my thoughts. I wouldn't be surprised if she actually could. "I know you think I was mean to him or left without responding. You think I left him hanging here this whole time. But I didn't. I flat-out told him no. That it wasn't right for me. I wanted more. I always have."

"Do you think your parents would've supported a marriage?"

"Are you kidding? My father would've driven us down to the justice of the peace that very night. He probably still would, if given the opportunity. He wanted me to stay. Wanted me to settle down. To become more like my mother, I guess." Her voice is tight, choked. She ducks underwater before I can see her expression.

I swim over to where she went under, looking around and finding her, the white of her underwear still visible. When she surfaces, I'm right in front of her.

And there's so much pain and hurt and guilt in her eyes.

"I'm sorry. I misjudged you," I tell her. "I

shouldn't have jumped to conclusions before I thought about things from your perspective. I wouldn't have wanted to be tied down into marrying someone at such a young age either. Some people can do that. Your sisters seem happy. And look at AJ and Lakelyn—they're blissful."

"But they went to college. They've lived more. I was only eighteen. I loved Trent, and he was a good high school boyfriend, but I knew deep down that he wasn't the one."

I draw closer to her. "You don't have to feel badly for following your dreams. Saying you've done well for yourself is an understatement."

There's a moment when our eyes meet, and my heart stops beating. I think, *This is it.* This is when we come back together. When we both decide to admit what's still between us.

Her lips part.

I want those lips.

I want to taste them. To lose myself in her the way I used to. When I stopped being me and she stopped being her and we would become … us, I guess. Something new, something bigger and better as partners than either of us was on our own.

"Carter …" she says breathlessly as she leans toward me.

And I know this is the moment.

She wraps her legs around me as I tread water, swimming us over to where I can stand and touch the bottom. Her lips reach mine. Our bodies are plastered together, my hands cupping her ass, and I'm aching for her.

"I knew I'd find you here!" Blake yells out.

I'd like to drown him right now.

Vale pulls back to look over my shoulder at her brother. "Your timing sucks."

"Yeah, well, that's what brothers are for."

I turn around and face Blake. "We've been going nonstop since we left LA. We just needed a few moments alone."

"Mom wouldn't be too happy if she knew you were hiding out here and necking while she needed help with the desserts. The rehearsal is in a few hours."

We swim over to the bank. Vale lets out a sigh and swims away from me.

Probably for the best. We might've gotten into trouble out there.

"She's right. Your timing does suck," I say to Blake.

"Just be glad I didn't take your clothes and ride off with them." He pedals away, laughing. "I was going to, just so you know. But I didn't because you're a pretty cool guy."

CHAPTER FIFTEEN
BLAH, BLAH, BLAH.

Vale

WE'RE IN THE formal gardens on the property. The gardens that were actually started by my grandmother and grew to what it is today. Which is basically breathtaking. Fortunately, we had an early spring this year, and the trees and flowers are in bloom.

At the end of the path we are on is the gazebo overlooking a small pond with a fountain. One that Grandma decided she wanted to add after seeing a hotel's water show in Vegas.

I thought my dad was going to fall off his chair. Needless to say, Grandma ended up settling for a smaller set of three fountains with colored lights that come on at night.

A few days after her project was complete, I asked if she was disappointed. She surprised me by saying no. Telling me that she'd asked for something bigger so that she got what she wanted. And then muttered something about my dad being a tight ass.

"Now, where's the maid of honor?" the wedding

planner says.

I hold up my hand with a smile. "Right here."

She nods, checking off something on her tablet with a stylus. "Perfect. Sister of the bride. You'll be after the flower girl and her wagon."

I wiggle my fingers at Sophie, who's so excited to have been given such a big job.

The planner lines the wedding party up.

First, AJ walks his mother down the aisle—a path of turf grass brought in for the occasion and placed over the pea gravel usually here. His father follows behind, and AJ seats them before taking his place at the gazebo altar.

Carter is lined up next. He holds out his arm to my grandmother, who gives his bicep a squeeze and smiles at him.

Needless to say, she's in seventh heaven.

"You certainly showed the rest of the boys around here a thing or two today," I hear her telling him.

"Thank you. I was hoping you'd be impressed," Carter says to her.

"Well, I was—you can be sure. If I were younger, I swear—"

"Mom." That would be my mother speaking. And she's aghast.

Carter looks over his shoulder at me, and we share a grin.

"You'll scare him off before they even have the

time to plan the wedding," my mother continues.

I'm pretty sure Grandma squeezes Carter's arm one more time before she takes her spot in the first row on the bride's side.

Carter then takes his place next to AJ.

My mother is next, escorted by my brother, Blake, who is actually behaving himself tonight.

They are followed by Lakelyn's bridesmaids and the other groomsmen—first my sisters with their respective spouses and then two pairs of their college friends.

Sophie, who was excited about her upcoming job as a flower girl, has been reduced to tears over the fact that her wagon isn't ready yet.

Thankfully, the wedding planner and Aunt Helen maneuver it in front of me before Sophie has a full-on meltdown.

"All right," the wedding planner says to Sophie, "you can walk down toward your mommy with the wagon."

"But I supposed to have babies!" she screeches.

"The babies will be here for the real wedding," I tell her, referring to Raine and Seth's twins, who will be in the wagon.

"I need babies to practice!" she yells.

I quickly grab two hymnals from the back pew and put them in the wagon. "You have to pretend they are the babies tonight since this is just practice."

"Just practice?" she asks.

"Yes, you have to make sure you can pull the wagon safely before we can put real babies in it."

She gives me a pout but takes the wagon's handle and makes her way to the front of the church. She only bangs into the pews and has to back up a couple of times, but she seems to get the hang of it by the end.

The wedding planner points to a spot. "You will stop here, so we can close the doors to allow the bride and her father to assemble without being seen. Wait until the flower girl gets situated and then make your processional."

I reach the gazebo and take my place.

"This is when the bridal march will start." She makes a motion with her hand, and it starts playing. "The guests will rise, and"—the wedding planner flings open pretend doors, where tomorrow, there will be a cased set of wooden doors standing there— "the bride will make her way to the front."

She's clapping her hands in time with their footsteps and counting out loud, making sure they go slow enough. I'm shocked my father hasn't told the woman he knows how to walk.

With all her precision, I halfway wonder if this woman has done fashion shows.

Lakelyn looks beautiful, and I can only imagine how she will be beaming tomorrow. She's carrying the huge ribbon bouquet that was made from all her shower wrappings and wearing her adorable jumpsuit. Her makeup is soft and pretty, and her hair is in bouncy curls.

"Lakelyn, you'll hand your bouquet to Vale."

My sister turns and pretends the ribbon bouquet is really heavy, grimacing and grunting.

"You're silly," I say, and we both giggle.

Until the planner scowls at us, and then we quit goofing around.

"This is when the minister will say, *We are gathered here today,* blah, blah, blah, love and whatever …"

I shouldn't have looked at Carter. He's struggling to hold back a laugh to the point where his eyes are watering.

"I wonder if she has a side business, writing sermons," Raine quips from behind us.

And that does it. A single bark of laughter erupts before I can stop myself, which makes Carter snort loud enough for us to all hear him. And the rest of the wedding party starts laughing too.

Well, except for my mother. I can practically feel the heat of her glare, but there's no helping it.

"I really hope you can behave yourselves tomorrow," the planner chastises but continues. "The officiant will pronounce you husband and wife—don't kiss; save it for the wedding—and you will make your exit."

Ignoring her instructions, AJ grabs my sister, dips her back, and gives her a big, loud smooch, which makes us all break out in laughter again.

They walk down the aisle, and then Carter takes a few steps to the center and meets me in the middle, holding out his elbow.

We're both still laughing. Actually, I'm practically gasping for air. I have no idea why this is all so funny.

Well, it was until Carter touches me.

Then, I'm lacking oxygen for a different reason.

He smiles at me and says, "So long as the minister doesn't say *blah, blah, blah, love and whatever*, I think we are good."

But all I'm thinking about is how I'm walking down the aisle with him.

And I kinda wish I were for real.

A CUTE STORY.

Carter

"I ALWAYS KNEW I would marry her." AJ looks over at Lakelyn with eyes filled with joy. "Been planning for this day since the summer I turned ten years old. When we first met. So, it isn't like I was nervous or anything to ask her to marry me."

"Until it actually was time," Lakelyn teases. "You

were a nervous wreck, and I couldn't figure out why. You'd just won your bowl game."

"For those of you here who don't know, I proposed to Lakelyn the night after our team won the national championship game. I considered doing it on the field after the game, but I wanted something a little more private, so I scheduled what she thought was a surprise hot air balloon ride for us."

"Thus the nervousness. He's afraid of heights!"

"But I did it for you, pumpkin," he says. "We were in Arizona, and the southwest is well-known for their balloon festivals. It was a little scary, being that high up off the ground in what was basically a wicker basket strapped to a parachute filled with hot air."

"When I first saw the balloon, the thought did cross my mind that it would be a cool place for a proposal. But I'd thought that many times before, and it hadn't happened. He was nervous. Pacing, checking his watch. Kept one hand in his pocket the whole time. I just kept trying to reassure him that we weren't going to plummet to our deaths."

AJ laughs. "Little did she know that I was freaking out because the photographers, who were supposed to be on the ride with us to capture the moment, were caught in traffic. And if we didn't take off soon, the lighting wouldn't be right, and … well, I just wanted it to be perfect."

I notice that Vale is mesmerized by their story even though I know she's probably heard it before.

And I realize that the photographer was like me. Stuck in traffic. Trying to get to a proposal. Although this one obviously happened, whereas mine didn't.

And I'm still stuck. Unable to move on without her.

"As soon as they arrived," Lakelyn says, "I was kind of bummed. I figured he'd want to propose in private. But, boy, what a view we had when we finally got up there. I had never been in Arizona before, and this was the most brightly colored sunset I'd seen. The view of all those colors over the mountains was just incredible."

"And just as the sky was ablaze with color, the photographers got out their gear, and I knew it was time. I took her hands and told her that I knew a lot was up in the air, concerning our lives together."

"Get it?!" Lakelyn screeches. "Isn't that the cutest thing ever?" She leans in and gives AJ a kiss.

I can't help but glance at Vale again. She's beaming and dabbing at her eyes.

I keep wondering if this could be us someday. *Will we laugh about the proposal that almost happened? Consider it just part of our love story?*

And these days, I don't know who I'm angrier with—her for kissing that guy or me for giving up on us so easily.

Either way, Ashlyn was right. I need to start fighting for Vale. I mean, whoever the guy was that night, he's certainly not here with her now.

I am.

She turns to me with a little shrug. "I'm a sucker for moments like this."

"And then I told her that I didn't want to do life without her," AJ continues, "that'd we go wherever the wind took us. It didn't matter as long as we were together."

"And then he goes, 'Lakelyn, do you remember that summer when we were ten and you taught me how to catch a frog?' And I was like, 'Uh, yeah.' And then he was like, 'And remember how you told me that you had to kiss the frog to see if he was really a prince?' And I was like, 'Yeah,' and then he was like, 'I was your frog. And now, I want to be your prince.' And I was like, 'Uh, okay.' But I didn't really get it. I thought he was talking about the draft because we didn't know where we were going to be living. And then I thought he was telling me this because he thought he was going to die via hot air balloon crash."

"Then, I got down on one knee," AJ continues. "Something that is no easy task for a big guy who is afraid of heights to do in a balloon basket with flames in the center. And the basket rocked. And I thought I was going to fall out, plummeting to my death before I got to ask her. To tell her how I felt. Nothing more than a little fear to get you high on life."

"More like a little of that ditch weed," Blake yells

out, referring to the marijuana that I'm sure grows wild around here.

"You should write greeting cards," Lakelyn fires back.

"And I asked her to marry me."

"And I said yes!" Lakelyn screeches happily.

"And here we are," AJ says. "So, don't laugh when you see the little frogs on our wedding cake."

Lakelyn's eyes get huge. "You didn't!"

But AJ just laughs.

Then, he raises his glass and says, "To my love. My life. My soon-to-be wife. I can't wait to marry you tomorrow."

Everyone at the rehearsal dinner joins him by toasting his bride.

"Now, let's eat!" he says.

"They have a cute story," I say to Vale.

"Yeah, they do. And such a long history."

I reach out and take her hand in mine. "Should we go get in line?"

She looks at the lines that have already formed, scrunches up her nose at me, and grins, pulling on my hand and leading me to the bar set up in the barn.

"This barn is really beautiful," I say. "The old brick and wood. The red exterior."

We order drinks from the bartender, he makes them and hands them to us, and then Vale gives me the lowdown.

"It is a showpiece. Original to the farm. Dad had it moved from its location near the acres of crops and the area of land where he grew up to this spot when they built the house here. It was falling apart a little, and they decided it would be a fun place to hang out, get together with friends, entertain clients. So, they restored it meticulously. The wood floors are not original though," she says. "But they were salvaged from old buildings in the area."

"Will the reception be here tomorrow too?" I ask.

"No, a big tent will be set up"—she pulls me out of the barn and gestures toward the large grassy area where we played football earlier—"over there. Although Mom prepared most of the food for last night and a few desserts for tonight, the rehearsal dinner and wedding reception will be fully catered. Guests will park over there." She points at another section of grass. "And then they'll get taken by horse-drawn carriages to the garden for the ceremony. It's going to be hectic around here tomorrow morning with everything getting set up."

"It sounds like it will be a beautiful wedding. Um, cheers," I say, clinking my glass against hers.

"What are we toasting to?" she asks, giving me a naughty grin. The kind that used to get her swept off her feet and either thrown in my pool or on my bed.

"How about to us?" I say and then immediately regret it when she asks the obvious question.

"To us?"

"Yes. And for now, let's leave it at that."

She nods at me and drains her drink.

We stop by the bar, grab two more, take them to our seats, and then get in line for food. It's a huge spread of barbecued meat, roasted potatoes, cheesy corn, baked beans, salad, and cornbread—among other things. I take a little of each meat—smoked sausage and chicken, beef brisket, and pork ribs. We're told there are sauces on the table and make our way back.

When we sit down, she turns to me, tears in her eyes again. "I feel really full, Carter."

"Full?" I say. "But you haven't even eaten yet."

"Not here." She touches her stomach. "Here," she says, placing her hand against my heart. "I didn't want to come home because of my father, but I'm so glad I did. It makes me happy to see my sister so happy. Do you know what I mean?"

"I felt the same way when Cade and Palmer got married. And Cash and Ashlyn. That feeling of being around people I love, watching one of them start something so full of promise."

It was during Cade's wedding just a few months ago that I had a ring I was planning to give the girl I loved.

I take her hand in mine, touch the ring on it, and think about how perfect it looks on her.

If she only knew.

AFTER WE'VE HAD our fill of dinner, Vale goes to raid the dessert table while I refill our drinks. When we meet back up, she has two plates full of brownies, pie, cupcakes, and cookies.

"What is that?" I ask, pointing to a bowl of what looks like pink whipped cream.

"Oh, this is my favorite. Pink fluff."

"Pink fluff? It doesn't look very healthy," I tease.

"You've never had it? Oh, Carter Crawford, you are missing out. It's practically a delicacy around here."

"It looks kind of disgusting," I admit.

"Don't knock it until you try it, city slicker," Mr. Martin says, cupping my shoulder from behind me. "We usually call it pink fluff salad, so we can get away with eating dessert for dinner."

He makes his way back to his seat, and I realize he just teased me.

Maybe he doesn't hate me after all.

So, I put a scoop on my plate.

SPEAKING OF THE BEDROOM.

Vale

"I'LL BE LUCKY if I fit into my dress tomorrow," Brooke says, sitting back in her chair. "Too much mac and cheese. Explain to me the purpose behind having a feast the night before the wedding when we have to look good in our dresses tomorrow."

"That's why I'm glad we chose the flowy ones." Raine very deliberately takes a forkful of macaroni and groans in pleasure as it crosses her lips.

"You're evil," Brooke hisses. She turns to Carter. "Do you have sisters?"

"I have one. Her name is Chloe. She's a jewelry designer who travels all over the world, looking for inspiration. She's brilliant and hilarious, and she won't let me or my brothers get away with anything."

"Meanwhile, we could try to keep up with Blake, but that would be a full-time job." Brooke looks over to where our brother is currently arm-wrestling one of the groomsmen.

"Yeah, I can see how that would start to become a profession." Carter gestures to his plate, looking my way. "This fluff stuff isn't half bad. Still have no clue exactly what's in it though."

"I told you it was good."

Our conversation is interrupted when my father clears his throat. He stands up, holding his wineglass in the air and says, "Everyone, if I could have your attention, I would like to make a toast."

"Uh-oh," Blake heckles.

I have to bite the inside of my cheek to keep from laughing.

Dad rolls his eyes at Blake but doesn't let it faze him. "Lakelyn, your mother and I discussed a few of the things we've done in our marriage that have kept us together all these years."

I want to roll my eyes, but I notice my mother is beaming.

"Much like the two of you, your mother and I have very different personalities. Speaking in football for AJ, we suggest you play off each other's strengths and block for each other when one is weak." He chuckles. "And one fun thing about being married means that if you want to get out of something, like, say, going to your mother's for dinner"—Dad smiles and looks at Grandma, who gives him her evil eye mixed with a smile—"you can now blame it on your spouse. It's like a *get out of jail free* card. Although, when you are newlyweds, you probably won't have all that much time out of the bedroom anyway."

My eyes go wide, as do my little sister's. She turns a shade of bright red, but AJ just takes her hand and chuckles nervously.

"Speaking of the bedroom, never go to sleep

angry," Dad continues. "And no matter what your best intentions are, AJ, you're probably going to always be wrong now." My dad gives AJ a smirk and raises his eyebrows. "Even when you are right. And I highly suggest you learn that when she says she is *fine*, she might be, but, son, you are anything but. Say you're sorry. Do right by each other. And share your love with others. And most importantly, we hope that you keep this place in your heart and know that wherever you go in life, we're proud of you, and you're always welcome at home."

The breath whooshes out of my lungs as I wonder why my father has never spoken those words to me. And the fact that he hasn't hurts more than I imagined.

After we raise our glasses, Grandma yells out, "And what about Carter?"

"What about him?" Dad asks her.

"Aren't you going to welcome him to the family?" Grandma says.

I notice that she and Aunt Helen have another full glass of peach wine in front of them.

"This weekend is not about us, Grandma," I say softly, hoping to shush her, while Carter nods in agreement.

"Hey! How about a double wedding?!" Blake heckles.

"Hey! I don't think so!" I chirp back, causing everyone to laugh.

To my utter amazement, my father raises his glass again. "Carter, we look forward to welcoming you into our family. I'm sorry it took Vale this long to come home, but the fact that she brought a good man with her takes the sting out just a bit. We're happy to have you here."

My heart practically stops beating. *Did my dad just give me a compliment? I chose a good man?*

I want to cry. Instead, I look at Carter, whose expression is unreadable.

"I think Dad killed him with kindness," Brooke whispers from behind her hand.

CHAPTER SIXTEEN
A LITTLE PRINCESS.

Carter

I NEED TO get away from the table for a minute.

This is all too much. The lying, the pride on the faces of Vale's parents. The expectations from everyone else.

The last thing I expected was to like everyone so much.

Outside, I find Sophie playing with her wagon, twirling in circles, and singing a song.

She sees me coming and runs over before jumping up and down in front of me. "I'm gonna be the flower girl!"

I act deeply impressed. "I saw you walk down the aisle earlier. That's a very important job."

"I know. And I'm four years old. So, I'm a big girl. I can do a big job."

"I agree."

"Wanna watch me practice?" She's already pulling me off to the side, where there's a wagon sitting in the middle of a bunch of toys. Probably to keep her occupied during the post-dinner party.

"I'd love to," I say, knowing I don't really have a choice.

I watch as she loads two baby dolls into the wagon. Then, she takes off running at top speed. The wagon bounces along, and eventually, one of the dolls goes flying out.

"No, baby!" She's so stern when she stops and turns around to pick up the doll. "No falling out. You've gotta hang on tight."

It's hard to keep a straight face. "Will your babies be in the wagon at the wedding?"

"Nope." She puts the doll back and pats its dress into place. "These are my practice babies. I pull real babies."

"Real … babies?"

"Baby Skylar and baby Sebastian."

"Your cousins?" I can only imagine her barreling down the aisle with real babies flying out of the wagon. They are either going to need helmets or be encased in bubble wrap. Possibly both.

"Yes!" She sashays over to me. "And I wear a beau-ti-ful dress and a princess crown of flowers." She sticks out one foot and wiggles it back and forth. "And sparkly pink shoes."

"Ooh."

"And I get my hair fixed, and I even get to wear makeup!" She claps her hands. "On my face!"

I wonder where she thinks she would've worn it

otherwise as I take a seat on the grass. "You know, being in a wedding is a big honor."

She nods, solemn.

"And pulling the babies is a big responsibility," I add.

"That's why the babies need to stay in the wagon since we have a big … re-pons-e-billy-tee." She sounds the word out slowly, carefully.

"Have you ever been to a wedding before?"

"No," she admits. "But I watched Mommy and Daddy's on TV."

I assume she means a video of their wedding. "Great. Did you notice that your mommy walked really slow down the aisle?"

"You have-ta walk slow, so everyone can see how pretty your dress is."

"And you're going to be wearing a beautiful dress, right? So, you need to walk slow too."

"So they can see my dress?"

"That's right."

She doesn't look convinced.

"Why don't you try it?" I set the babies up in the wagon, including the one that now has a grass stain on its forehead. "Pretend I'm at the gazebo and you're walking down the aisle. Stand up straight and tall, the way your mommy did, and take your time."

She must interpret this as *go wild* since she whips the wagon around in a circle.

Both babies fall out this time.

"Shit!" she mutters in the most adorable way ever.

I have to cover my mouth with my hand to stifle a laugh as she tosses the dolls inside, so they're lying on top of each other.

"Babies, stay!" she orders them.

She looks at her left hand. "I supposed to have flowers. I need practice flowers." It's so cute, the way she crosses her arms over her chest and puffs out her lower lip.

"Let's pick some flowers then," I suggest.

She takes me by the hand and leads me over to a flowerbed in front of the barn. "I want this big pink one," she says, pointing. "And this yellow one. And these little pink ones. And two of these pretty red ones."

The girl knows what she wants.

I carefully pick a handful, forming it into a bouquet. There's a roll of twine hanging off a peg just to the left of the barn door and a pair of scissors hanging off another peg.

They're probably there for just this purpose, I think as I cut off a length of twine and wind it around the mini bouquet.

"So pretty!" she whispers, taking them with an awed expression before running for the wagon to start practicing again.

Except once she repeats her stance, she shakes her head. "I need the flowers for my hair."

"This is only practice. You don't need—"

"I. Need. Flowers. For. My. Hair," she demands. It's like a tremor warning of an impending earthquake.

"Gotcha." I hurry back to the flowers and cut a few small blooms. Working them into a crown is a little beyond my expertise, so I tuck them into her hair instead.

"Now, I'm ready," she says. "You sit."

I sit because I'm almost afraid not to at this point.

"Babies, you sit too," she orders.

When they don't since they're fake and everything, she sighs like an exhausted caretaker and repositions them.

Finally, everything's perfect.

She takes the wagon handle in one hand, clutching her bouquet in the other, and takes a step.

Then stops.

I hold my breath.

"There's no music."

"Uh, hang on." I pull out my phone, choose a song off a playlist full of old jazz, and hit play.

Finally, she begins her walk down the fake aisle. When she gets to me, she says, "Say I look beautiful."

"The flower girl looks so lovely," I stage whisper with added astonishment. "What a beautiful dress. I'm so glad she's walking slow enough that I can see it. And her shoes just sparkle."

She nods and continues walking slowly, head held high.

When she gets to the end, she turns around and looks at the dolls. "The babies didn't fall out! Good babies!" She leaps into the air, waving the bouquet around.

"You know why? Because you walked slow."

She runs across the grass and leaps into my lap, flinging her arms around my neck. "I practice some more. You watch."

"Okay."

"Carter?" Vale says from behind me, making me jump. She then says, "Hey, Sophie, why don't you go practice again? I need Carter to help me for a minute."

When I get up, Sophie reminds me, "I need music."

I set my phone in the wagon and leave the playlist running before turning to Vale.

There are tears shimmering in her eyes.

"What's wrong?" I ask, immediately pulling her into my arms.

She smiles. "You're going to be a great dad someday."

I can't help but smile. "She's a little princess, isn't she?"

"Half-princess, half-hellion." She laughs. "A lot like me, apparently."

"I can see that. The girl does know what she

wants."

"Which is where she and I differ."

"You don't know what you want?" I ask, searching her eyes and wondering where this is going.

"I've never known for sure what I wanted. It's more like I know what I don't want. I didn't want what my dad wanted for me. I didn't want to be tied down with a husband and kids. I wasn't ready to live up to family expectations."

"But now?"

She sighs, looking deep into my eyes.

"Kiss!" Sophie yells. "I now pronounce you married!"

I don't hesitate. I mean, I already know we'd better do what Sophie wants.

And it's not like I haven't been dying to properly kiss Vale again since the one on the porch.

I gently cup her cheeks in my hands and slowly lean in, planting my lips on hers. Her body melts into mine as fire spreads through me.

I shove my tongue into her mouth, deepening the kiss and tightening our embrace.

"Okay, stop kiss!" Sophie yells.

I open my eyes to find her marching down the path toward us, pointing.

She's probably right. Any more of this, and things might have gotten a little too hot for public consumption. And most definitely wouldn't have stayed G-rated.

"We'd better do as she says," I whisper after reluctantly pulling my lips away.

That doesn't mean the moment's over. Vale is still in my arms, and the two of us might as well be in our own world.

The truth of what she wants shines in her eyes.

She wants all the things she thought she didn't.

And the way she looks at me gives me hope that she might even want them with me.

TEST THE SHOCKS.

"Where are you taking me?"

"You'll see," I say, throwing on a sweater against the chilly night air. "Shh." I have to look over my shoulder a few times just to be sure no one is watching.

"What's with all the secrecy?"

"I want to show you something. But if you keep talking, we'll get busted."

"Got it." Carter shuts up and lets me lead him away from the barn, past the house, and down to a shed—where I find exactly what I was looking for. A four-wheeler.

"What are you doing?" Carter watches me, laughing, as I get behind the wheel.

"I'm getting away from prying eyes and young ears for a little while. You feel like coming with or what?" I give him my best sexy look.

And it works. He's next to me in no time, and soon, we're cruising away toward the fields.

"Where are we going?" he calls out over the wind rushing past us.

"Away!" I don't stop until we're far enough from the house and the party that there's hardly more than soft music drifting from that direction.

I brake, shut off the engine, and then turn toward Carter.

Carter, who I've been lusting after for much longer than the past few days.

Who looks and smells so damn good.

Who just stole my heart back there with how patient and sweet he was with Sophie.

"I need to tell you something," I blurt out.

"What?" he asks, a playful little smile tugging at his lips.

I lean in, taking his face in my hands, and kiss him the way I wanted to back there.

Carter responds, pulling me closer up and onto his lap so that I'm straddling him. His hands, his lips, the way he nips my earlobe before devouring my neck and shoulder are so familiar, but at the same time, it all feels so new and exciting.

"Vale," he moans as his hands slide up and down my back before gripping my ass and grinding me against his jeans.

"I need you," I tell him, my hands undoing his belt and then his zipper. "Now."

It takes a little maneuvering for him to get a condom out of his wallet, but we manage without either of us falling off the vehicle.

He wants this as much as I do, which only makes me more determined to have him.

There's nothing romantic or sweet about it. We take each other hard and fast, groaning into each other's mouths as our tongues tangle, the vehicle bouncing under us.

I needed this. I needed him so badly.

"Yes … yes …" I close my eyes and bury my face in his neck, breathing in his cologne and his sweat and whatever makes him Carter. Whatever makes him irresistible, whatever makes my heart come back to him again and again.

Our bodies move together, making the four-wheeler creak.

"Wow," I say.

He chuckles against my hair. "Yeah. Wow."

"You did tell me on the porch that we'd *finish this later.*"

"I'd say we just did," he says with a grin. His mouth is at my neck, running lazy kisses up it, but I can feel his lips form into a smile. "I only want to know one thing. Why the four-wheeler?"

"It was there, and I figured it would be more comfortable than a bicycle. And if I had taken you upstairs, I'm pretty sure everyone would have known. Either someone would have seen us sneaking up there or they'd have heard me calling out your name."

That earns me a slow smile. "Would they? You were pretty quiet just now."

I take him by the collar and pull him to me. "Who said we were finished? Let's really test the shocks on this baby."

CHAPTER SEVENTEEN
GARDEN OF EDEN.

Carter

"I THINK I liked the four-wheeler better." I roll off Vale and onto my back, a blanket between it and the floor.

"Me too. It's hard to be quiet when I'm with you. Especially since it's been so long."

I'm more than okay with doing it on the floor. Against the wall. In the shower. So long as I can soak in as much of her as possible for as long as possible. Because this is different. It's not just hot hook-up sex like on the four-wheeler. Here, I'm making love to her. And I'm hoping my body will tell her what my words have yet to.

She snuggles close to me. "You'd better take it easy on me, or I won't be able to make it up the aisle tomorrow."

"We aren't anywhere near our record yet," I tease. Although it's not a teasing matter. I've never wanted a woman so much or so often as I do her.

"Hmm. That's true." She giggles softly, running

her leg over mine. "But you hadn't been in the farm games like you were today."

"True, but I am up for the challenge if you are. What are you up to now? Four times?"

"Five, but who's counting?" She stretches and purrs like a cat.

If I have it my way, we'll double that by morning.

"This is going to sound ridiculous after the huge dinner we had earlier," I say, "but I'm starving. Want to go get something to eat?"

She snuggles back up to me, sexily sliding a finger down my chest. "Well, we certainly have worked up an appetite."

Soon, we're in our robes, tiptoeing down the stairs. This is the quietest the house has been since I got here. We happily find the fridge packed with leftovers.

"What do you want?" she asks, holding the door open.

"Oh," I say, rubbing my stomach.

This causes her to giggle. She goes up on her tiptoes and kisses my cheek. "All of it, right?"

I shake my head. All I can think about is getting her back upstairs. I slide my hand inside her robe, grazing her naked form underneath.

"I thought you were hungry," she teases, nipping at my lip.

"For you." I glance at the kitchen island.

She follows my gaze. "Really?"

"Wouldn't be the first time," I say, recalling how things usually went when we were supposed to be making dinner together.

"It would most definitely be the first time in my family's kitchen," she counters and pulls away from me. "Get some food out. I'm starving. Then, we'll talk about the island."

I reluctantly let go of her and survey the containers in the refrigerator, filling my arms with brisket, pulled pork, coleslaw, and sauce. I'm thinking the buns are probably in the pantry.

I turn around to find her sitting up on the kitchen island. Her robe is gaping open in the front, and does she ever look beautiful.

I let out a whoosh of air, wondering how I got so lucky.

Needless to say, I quickly discard the food and slip my hand inside the robe, landing on her waist. "Maybe we could take it back upstairs?"

"As much as I would like that," she says with a sexy grin, "I really am starving."

And I agree with her. I give her a deep kiss, remove my hand, and then get serious about making sandwiches. "There are a lot of leftovers."

"There's more out in the garage fridge," she says, plopping a pile of coleslaw on each of our plates. "But I'm sure by the time everyone takes some home, there will be a lot less. Not to mention, the size of the sandwiches my father likes to eat. It'll get gobbled up fast."

I look around the room. "You'd never know there was a huge party here. Does your mom ever sleep?"

"I hope she's sleeping now," she says with a smirk.

She pops some mac and cheese in the microwave while I find the rolls.

"She's practically superhuman," I tell her. "I can see where your drive and energy come from."

She smiles, though there's a tightness to it, like I said the wrong thing. "I wish she had more of an opportunity to use her gifts."

"It seems like she's using them pretty well now," I offer.

"You know what I mean."

I don't reply, just nod and fix myself a sandwich. "Do you not think her life is fulfilling?"

"How could it be?"

"You don't have to have the same goals as her. Or even like to do the same things. I think you're extraordinary just the way you are. But it takes all kinds of people to make a world. If she gets joy out of running the household, looking after her grand-babies, and hosting Sunday suppers for whoever feels like dropping by, good for her. You can't look at her life through your eyes."

I can tell she knows what I mean, but she doesn't

want to listen. She has ideas about what her mother's life is like or what role her father plays, and it'll take more than a late-night chat over leftovers to change her mind.

I can't help but wonder whether things would be better for her, easier, if she learned to let go of the preconceived notions she seems to have about her parents. But at the same time, those ideas shaped her life and helped make her who she is now—which I'm coming to realize is someone who is afraid to dream of all the things she wants, for fear that she will end up like them.

"Oh," I say once we have our sandwiches made and the side dishes reheated, "do you think there is any more of that pink stuff left?"

She opens the fridge, searches around, and then pulls out a container. "Score!" When she sets it on the table and plops a spoonful on my plate, she says, "I told you, you would like it."

"You're right. I had preconceived notions about it. Amazing what you learn when you give things a chance."

"Why do I feel like you're talking about something else?"

"I dunno," I tease.

I figure she'll have a comeback, but I notice she's not smiling. Instead, she's looking down at her hand. The engagement ring is there, still shining, and I hate the fact that she'll give it back to me when we go home.

I want to broach the subject, but with all she's going through with her family, I know now is not the time.

"What's in this stuff anyway?" I ask, putting a glob of fluff on her lips before licking it off.

She looks up at me in surprise and starts laughing.

"Shh," I say.

But it's too late. A light comes on in the hall, and her father barrels down the stairs. He isn't carrying a gun, thankfully, but he looks ready for a fight.

"What are you two doing down here?" he asks. "You should be asleep. Big day today."

"It's my fault, sir," I tell him. "I woke up to use the bathroom and realized I was starving."

"Thought you didn't like the fruit salad," he says, taking the container off the table and grabbing a spoon.

"What's in it anyway? Or do I really want to know?"

"Cool Whip, mandarin oranges, crushed pineapple, maraschino cherries, and cherry Jell-O," Vale replies. "I mean, it's got fruit."

Her dad takes a big bite and says, "You can't forget the candied pecans for the top. Those are my favorite. It's like the Garden of Eden in one dish."

We clean up the kitchen, her father goes back to bed, and I slide my arms around her waist.

"How about we try to break our record now that we've refueled?" I nibble her neck while my hands take a tour of her lush body.

And I know that fluff isn't the Garden of Eden. It's her. The perfect place.

She lets out a throaty chuckle. "I think I'm up for the challenge."

YOU'RE BLUSHING.

SOMEONE IS KISSING me.

Not my mouth. My body.

Kisses rain down on my chest and then roll across my stomach.

I slowly open my eyes. My hands find him first. His shoulders, his neck. I wind my fingers through his hair, sighing as his mouth moves lower.

This is more sex than we've ever had in such a short time frame, but I'm certainly not complaining. I have to bite my lip to hold back a moan when his tongue sweeps over my inner thigh, so achingly close to its destination.

"Shh ..." he teases.

I look down and find him grinning devilishly at

me.

"Don't want anyone to hear."

"There's already a lot of noise coming from downstairs," I say. "Maybe they'll drown us out."

I know I should get out of bed right now. We both should. It's the big wedding day, and our schedules are jam-packed. I glance at my phone on the bedside table, seeing that, technically, we have about twenty minutes before we have to meet in the kitchen.

So, instead of getting up, I move my body so that his tongue is where I like it.

Then, I'm swept away as I lose myself in everything that is Carter Crawford.

When our desires are fully fulfilled, I can't help it. I start giggling.

"What just happened is not something to laugh about," Carter says.

"No, but trying to be quiet so my whole family couldn't hear us kind of is. I don't know if I can go down and face all of them, knowing what we did in this room all night. I'll probably be blushing."

He starts to get up, and then he leans back down and kisses my forehead. "You're blushing right now."

"I'm *flushed* right now. There's a big difference," I lie, even though I'm sure I am.

But then he heads into the bathroom and turns on the shower.

I follow him into the room, make sure both the

door to the hall and the door to my bedroom are locked, and then peek behind the shower curtain.

"Thought we should share since we're tight on time and all."

"That's a good plan," he says, bringing his lips down onto mine.

CHAPTER EIGHTEEN
FILLED WITH LOVE.

Vale

BACKSTAGE AT A fashion show is always organized chaos.

What's happening on the farm today in order to get it ready for the wedding appears to be just plain chaos. The wedding planner is jogging from one spot to another. And I understand now why she's wearing running shoes with her tweed pastel suit.

But just like a fashion show, once it starts, everything will go off without a hitch. And anything that does go wrong, well, you just have to roll with it.

The good news is that it's an absolutely gorgeous, warm spring day. I step out onto the balcony that overlooks the backyard, outdoor entertaining space, and the formal gardens, and I take in a few deep breaths, sucking in the clean country air.

As to be expected, the gardens and gazebo where the ceremony will take place are a hive of activity. Chairs are stacked up, waiting to be placed into rows. The beautifully ornate oak doors we'll walk through are already set up, as is the table outside that will hold the guest book and photos of the happy couple. There is a team of florists taking pastel flowers from buckets and stringing them into garlands to decorate the outside of the gazebo, and a big chandelier is being hung from the center of it.

The aisle of grass is marked with one chair on each side to show where each row starts, and punctuating the end of the row is a mason jar tied with pale ribbons, hanging from garden hooks. I know these will be filled with lush pink peonies.

I take a sip of the coffee I brought out with me and check the time again. The bride's attendants are all supposed to meet in about forty minutes in my parents' dining room, which is being transformed into a salon by a hair and makeup team who will get us glammed up for the occasion.

I look up at the sky—not a cloud in it—and remember so many days I spent here as a kid. I had a really great childhood. Loving parents. Close siblings. A close-knit, small-town community.

I think about all the beautiful places I've traveled in the world. All the places I have lived in since I left the farm, and I realize that no matter where I am, no matter how far I roam, this will always be where I grew up.

It's a shocking thought.

The fact that I would still see it that way. That I could actually picture myself having children someday. Bringing them here to see my family.

I let out a sigh.

If my dad hadn't ruined things between us when I left, I know I would have come back to visit. To spend time with my siblings. I might have even built a little cottage on some nearby land. A place I could come to unwind. Relax.

I never seem to stay in one place very long. Never owned a home of my own. Always rented something, usually set up by my agents to coordinate with where I need to be to do a photo shoot or walk runways. I've stayed in a million hotels. Actually, not that many. Sounds crazy, but I have kept a key from every hotel room I've ever stayed in. In Europe, where they still use actual keys, I begged or bought them. I have a whole basket of them. The closest thing I have to a permanent location is a Santa Monica office that basically functions as a very large closet. My assistant works there on a daily basis and is in charge of packing everything I might need. Between her and my stylist, I never have to worry about what to wear.

And I like it that way.

But when I stayed with Carter at his house on the beach, I couldn't help but wish I had a place like that. Or better yet, could live there with him.

I need to figure out what I want out of life.

My dad's toast last night hurt me. But it also surprised me. He made it sound like he and Mom functioned as a team. And Mom smiled—genuinely smiled—like she agreed.

It makes me wonder if I could have been wrong. About my parents. About not wanting things like a partner or children because I was afraid I would lose myself in them.

Like I thought my mom did.

I need to get my head in the game. Focus on my sister's wedding. Then, maybe later, I can think more about my future.

I make my way back inside, surprised to find the kitchen empty. The glam team is setting up in the dining room, but no one in the wedding party is around, so I go out onto the front porch.

More activity is happening out here. The clear-roofed tent is already set up. A caterer's van is in front of the barn, as is a rental company van that is being unloaded. I walk over there and see what's in them. I've seen all of my sister's dream boards, but I am not completely sure what she ended up choosing. I can see floral china, gold chargers and flatware, and pink wine goblets, all spread out on temporary tables in the barn. There are more florists stringing garlands on a bunch of chandeliers. And another group is building what appears to be a wall of flowers.

Inside the tent is also really busy. And it's where I find my mother. Up on a ladder.

"What are you doing?" I ask her.

It's obvious they hired companies to do all of this for her.

She hands me a coil of twinkle lights. "Can you help us string these up the way Brooke has done over there?" She points to my sister, who's hooking lights to the tent's support poles and then across the perimeter. Which I'm confused by because there are already lights running from the sides up to the center of the tent, creating a canopy of light.

"I see the other lights are hung. Why don't you let the company setting it up do that?"

"The tent company has already left," she huffs. "I knew I should have checked every detail before I signed off on it. They did the ceiling but neglected to do the sides. Your sister wants the place to glow. The crazy thing is, they left the lights, just didn't hang them."

"Do you want me to call them? Get them to come back?"

My mother sighs at me. "Do you think I would be standing on a ladder, doing this myself, on the morning of my daughter's wedding, if I hadn't already tried that? I'm not an idiot, you know. I've been running this household, this farm, and planning numerous large events for years. Your sister talked me into hiring a wedding planner so that I could relax, but as you can see, she's nowhere to be found."

"She's in the garden, helping the florists with the ceremony stuff. Probably since that's first and all."

"Don't get sassy with me, Vale," she says. "I'm under enough stress as it is already. Either grab some lights and help or go somewhere else."

I leave my mother's side, pushing my hand against the side of my jeans so that I don't pull it up into a mock salute and really piss her off, and go pick up a string of lights. It's a long, horizontal string that has multiple strings of lights that hang vertically from it.

"Where are the boys?" Raine asks me as I climb up a stepladder. "I've tried texting Seth, but he hasn't replied."

"I'm not sure. I know Dad and AJ wanted to show Carter around before they hit the golf course."

"It doesn't seem fair," Brooke says. "Here we are, setting things up. Then, we have to sit through hair and makeup. What do they do? They take a tour of the farm and go golfing."

"Maybe they need to relax after all that cornhole and flag football," Raine teases. "Poor, tired babies."

I can think of one man who most certainly worked hard yesterday, and I'm not talking about the games.

"We should call them," I suggest.

"Already tried," Lakelyn says, joining us. She lowers her voice to a whisper. "No one is answering. Honestly, Mom is freaking out over this. There's no reason it has to be done right this minute when the reception is hours away."

"Well, I'm assuming she doesn't want to do it once she's all ready," I suggest, surprised that I'm standing up for her.

"The lights are pretty," Lakelyn says.

"They are, and everything should be pretty today. And you, little miss, should be in the house, feet up, mimosa in hand, doing nothing but dreaming of your honeymoon."

"We're not going on a honeymoon for a while. The draft is coming up. And I have finals."

"Okay, so when you go on a honeymoon *later*, where are you going?" I ask her.

"No idea. AJ is in charge of it. And he says it depends on how big his signing bonus is. We want to get moved to our new city, then go on our honey-moon. Relax and enjoy ourselves after all the stress of that is over." She shakes her head and smiles. "Lots of change coming our way."

"Change is exciting," I say.

"Does that mean we might see you around here more often?" Brooke asks.

"Maybe," I say, but I'm not sure I mean it.

Mom comes over to where we are chatting. "This isn't going fast enough. Call your father."

"He's off with the boys, and they have golf soon."

She gives me a look. "I absolutely don't care what they have planned. These lights are going to get hung. Now."

"Uh, I'll call them," I say as she exits the tent in a huff.

JUST LIKE ME.

Carter

"SEE THIS HERE piece of equipment?" Mr. Martin says to me as he gestures toward a large combine. "It's always funny, seeing them Hollywood types bragging about their fancy Lambos and Ferraris like they're better than everyone else. And I got this sitting here, which cost more than both, and I only use it once a year. You look like the Ferrari type, Carter."

"I don't have a Ferrari, sir," I respectfully reply.

"He's got a Bentley," AJ clarifies with a grin, and I find myself wishing we hadn't talked about my toys on the way back from the bachelor party. I didn't think he'd even remember.

"Same difference," Mr. Martin says.

"Not really, sir," AJ counters. "A Bentley is more subtle. Carter isn't about flash regardless of his net worth. Though I've heard he has his own plane—a pretty new Gulfstream. Now, that cost a lot more than this fine piece of machinery."

"What is this, some pissing match?" Mr. Martin scowls at me.

"With all due respect, sir," AJ says, "you started it."

The man starts laughing. "I guess I did. But what

do you expect? He got engaged to my daughter and hadn't asked for my permission." He cuffs AJ on the shoulder. "At least you did it the right way."

"I'm sorry, sir," I say. "I wasn't raised that way. The engagement was … never mind."

"No, tell me."

I find myself blurting out the truth, the story I've never admitted to anyone, not even my own family. I told them I chickened out. That the timing wasn't right.

"I was crazy about Vale from the moment I met her, but with our busy work schedules, our relationship was what I'd guess you'd call casual dating. We would hang out whenever we could. I went to Fashion Week with her and invited her to join me on our family vacation. It felt like things could be more, but after that, we just fell back into our old routine. I was worried if I pushed, I might lose her. And in that process, I might have given off an air of ambivalence about it.

"I wanted to prove my love, so I had a ring made. I had every intention of calling or meeting you before I proposed, but then my older brother got married at Christmastime. I was inspired by their love, and I wanted that for myself.

"Vale invited me to her New Year's Eve party in New York. I told her that I wasn't sure if I could make it because I wanted to surprise her by showing up and proposing at midnight as the ball dropped.

Which, in retrospect, was probably not the smartest thing I've ever done."

"Why not?" AJ asks.

"Well, when I got there, unfortunately, she was kissing another man." I take a deep breath. "I took it as a sign. Turned around and left."

"Tucked your tail and ran away? Huh," Mr. Martin says. "That, I wouldn't have expected from you. I saw you win the Heisman. Watched you play in the Rose Bowl against my beloved Hawkeyes. You were one hell of a quarterback. Expected to go first round in the draft. Picked our defense apart. The score was embarrassing for us. You were ranked first. We were second. But it was no contest. Even after you were carted off the field."

He turns to AJ again. "That's why I worry about you going pro. You could get injured and not be able to provide for your family. What will you do then? Why not just work at the bank with me? Or on the farm, like Seth? Or maybe one of the dealerships?"

"We've had this conversation before," AJ says. "And you know my signing bonus alone should be enough that I will be able to take care of your daughter financially for the rest of our lives, no matter what happens.

"Carter here is a good example of that. He could have gone pro after his junior year and probably should have, but he stayed in school and got his degree, just like I did. I could have been hurt. Hell, I could have gotten in a car wreck or flipped my four-wheeler.

"We never know what will happen. But I love playing football. I'm good at it. It's my passion. And it's what I want to do with my life." He pauses and looks his future father-in-law straight in the eye. And I have an immediate respect for the kid.

"Your daughter, who I love and would do just about anything for, is fully supportive of this endeavor."

"You still planning to use your uncle in your contract negotiations?" Mr. Martin asks him.

My ears perk up in surprise, but I keep my mouth shut.

"My dad is pretty adamant about it," AJ says. "He's a tight ass, like you, says I'd be stupid to give a percentage to an agent when my uncle could review my contract."

Mr. Martin shakes his head. "I might be a tight ass, but there's one thing I never cut corners on, and that's a good lawyer." He sticks a piece of hay in his mouth and turns to me. "What do you think, Carter? You're supposed to be some highfalutin sports agent, which is really just a very specialized attorney, right?"

"Yes, I suppose that's right. I do a lot more for our clients than a typical attorney though."

"Like what?" AJ asks.

I know this is more for Mr. Martin's benefit than his since we've already had this conversation. He wants to show his future father-in-law my worth—and maybe help influence his own father somehow.

"I consider myself a hub on the wheel of my clients' businesses. I work with and recommend financial advisors so they can safely invest their money and accountants who specialize in the industry and understand the best tax shelters. I always help my clients get settled into the city they are drafted or traded to. I've dealt with crazy ex-girlfriends, money-grubbing relatives, paternity suits, and stalkers. I have a personal relationship with those I represent."

"He's also Danny Diamond's agent," AJ adds.

"I hear Danny's an upstanding man," Mr. Martin says.

"He is," I agree.

"Most agents go for any client they can get but not Carter," AJ adds. "He has a small but highly successful group of clients."

"How do you do that?" Mr. Martin says, tilting his head at me.

"Because of all the things that I mentioned above, that means I get involved with my clients on a personal level. So, I choose people that *I* mesh with. Good men and women—on and off the field."

"So, why aren't you working with AJ here?" He kicks a little dirt in AJ's direction. "I don't like most people, but I do like him."

"Because I was told he already has representation," I say simply.

"Do you think hiring his uncle is a smart move?" Mr. Martin asks me.

"No, I don't. But it's not my decision to make."

"Dad," Vale calls out from behind me, her voice sounding stressed.

I turn around and am struck by how beautiful she looks.

I know she thinks she doesn't belong here, yet she looks so at home. Her hair is down and curling at the ends. The light jeans she's wearing fit her snugly. A white lace top is tied in a knot at the waist. The whole outfit is modest, but it certainly doesn't hide her sexiness.

She's moving toward us when her dad says, "We just heard that Carter was going to propose to you on New Year's Eve but got there and found you necking with another man. How is it you're engaged now? What happened in between?"

Vale looks at me, her eyes wide, but she quickly hides it and says, "We'll have to talk about that later. Mom needs your help in the tent before she has a breakdown over some twinkle lights not getting strung."

"Well then, we'd better hop to it. When that woman sets her mind to something, there's no denying her. She keeps me on a tight rope." He turns to AJ. "You'd better head to the golf course. We don't want you to accidentally see Lakelyn and jinx things."

"No, sir. I'd be in big trouble."

"We'll be right behind you," Vale says to her dad. She looks equally shocked at both what he said about her mother and what he said about the proposal.

She drags me away, but the second we are out of earshot of AJ, she stops and asks, "Is what he said really true?"

"Yeah, it is actually," I admit. "Cade and Palmer had gotten married, and I planned this big surprise moment. I timed it perfectly. Literally, I would have pulled you into my arms at midnight, kissed you, and then dropped down on one knee. Just like in your dream."

"Why didn't you tell me?! I didn't think you were coming to the party. I thought you'd stood me up. I was sad. Pissed actually. I was kissing some random guy. It didn't mean anything."

"His hands looked very comfortable all over your ass. He wasn't *just* some random guy," I counter.

"Fine, I mean, we had hooked up before, but I wasn't serious about him."

"Just like me, apparently."

And even though I don't want to, I walk away. Just like I did then. Because it hurts too much.

Especially after last night.

CHAPTER NINETEEN
CANDIDATE FOR SAINTHOOD.

Carter

I SUCK AT golf right now, and it's a game I take pride in. But my head and my heart are aching so badly that I can barely concentrate. After the sex we shared last night, I hoped we maybe could start over. But then I stupidly told her dad the truth about the proposal, and he turned right around and told her.

And I got mad all over again.

"I swear, I'm usually much better at this." I run a hand over the back of my neck, wincing at my terrible performance.

AJ snickers. "You look nervous. Like you're the one getting married later."

"How in the world are you so cool right now?"

His game has been impeccable.

He shrugs, looking out over the rolling expanse of green all around us. "That's easy. Today makes the most sense out of anything I've ever done in my life."

He pulls a couple of beers from the cooler on the

back of the golf cart, handing one to me. Blake and Seth are a hole behind us while Jake is in the middle of setting up a putt.

"I've gotta say, when you showed up here, the first thing I thought was that you were here to sign me. But you don't seem interested."

"What makes you feel that way?"

He shrugs. "We talked when you first got here, and you were helpful. You didn't have that whole shark thing going on. If you know what I mean."

I do, so I nod.

"Then, we had that conversation earlier today. I think you convinced Mr. Martin. I'm sure he feels a lot better now, if only for Lakelyn's sake. You explained what you do, but you weren't pushing. You weren't trying to sell yourself."

"I don't push, AJ. I don't have to. All that needs to be done is to explain what I bring to the table. I like working with smart people who understand my value." I give him a nudge. "Besides, that's not why I'm here."

He still looks troubled. "It's just that I'm worried my uncle will be insulted, which will piss my dad off. He's only interested in me keeping more money."

"Or, with all due respect, your uncle could put up a fuss, and a team will get so sick of dealing with someone who's not professional that you'll still be waiting to sign when the season has started. Seen that happen many times. Also, teams have salary caps. He can't negotiate that much on your earnings. But honestly, it's not what's in the contract that concerns me. It's what might *not* be."

"Like what?"

"For instance, standard contracts don't always contain clauses for what happens if you get hurt. What if you're placed on injured reserve? What if they try to fire you? With cause or without. Will there be performance bonuses? Are they team or individual?" I have to chuckle in sympathy at the frown he's wearing now.

"I'm not trying to overwhelm you. I've just seen situations like this play out before. And it typically isn't good for the player. And I'm only scratching the surface. There are so many variables in each sport, even across individual teams. I've dealt with those things either through my own clients or I've heard about them through the agency I'm affiliated with. What you're getting with a good agent is all that experience."

I lower my voice a little, remembering our earlier conversation. "I know you said your dad believes you're a fool to give a percentage to an agent, but here's a question for him. *How much money are you leaving on the table if you sign a contract that doesn't cover everything?* Bonuses, injury pay, all of it could be lost. Not to mention, the other situations I described earlier. Getting my clients out of trouble, dealing with fans who don't know what boundaries mean, helping them manage their money." I give him a smile. "Every one of my clients will tell you that I'm worth every penny."

"As far as I'm concerned, you're the guy I want. But it feels very complicated."

"Then, uncomplicate it. You have to stop playing the role of a child and stand up for yourself, your wife, and your future family. It's great to go to people you trust for advice, but ultimately, it's your decision, and you and Lakelyn are the ones who have to live with the consequences of that decision."

He takes a pull of his beer. "Lakelyn didn't want this big of a wedding. I'm not complaining, and I know she wouldn't either. The Martins have been so generous. But it's because it's what they wanted. Not what she did."

"Does that bother you?" I ask.

"Yeah, it does. I want her to have everything she dreams of. Not have her dreams forced on her."

"Then, it sounds like you'd better start being a man. If you want me to represent you, I will. But it's your decision to make, and I won't pressure you."

"Vale's lucky to have found you." He laughs. "Or maybe I'm lucky you found Vale. Either way, glad you're going to be part of the family."

It's in that moment that I realize I should not take him as a client. I pride myself on my integrity. And I'm lying to him right now. Not the best way to start off a relationship.

Why didn't I say no to her when she showed up at my doorstep?

Probably because she was literally down on her knees.

And because I'm still in love with her.

And probably because I'm an idiot.

"What's the holdup?" I can see Blake waiting to tee off, shouting with his hands cupped around his mouth. "Do we have to play through?"

"Man"—Jake laughs, joining us—"I feel sorry for the girl who thinks she can handle him one day. Poor girl will have to be a candidate for sainthood."

I have to bite my tongue to stop from saying something of that effect about all the Martins, but since she showed up at my door, I don't exactly qualify for sainthood myself.

TIME YOU COME HOME.

I GO BACK to the tent in a daze and take a seat in the corner, hiding behind a plant. I need a minute. I'm still shocked over two things.

Carter was going to propose?

And my mom has my dad on a tight rope?

Am I just an idiot? Have I been wrong all this time about my parents' relationship?

The answer to that question is answered pretty quickly when my father marches into the tent with the wedding planner.

"Sarah," he says to my mother, "come down off that ladder, please."

My mom puffs out her chest, clearly irritated by the whole situation.

Dad takes her hand. "I've taken care of everything."

Mom looks at the wedding planner with a shrewd eye. The woman practically recoils.

"I'm sorry for the misunderstanding about the lights on the sides of the tent. I've spoken to the tent company—"

My father coughs.

"Well, I spoke to them after your husband did. Needless to say, they are sending a crew that will arrive in less than thirty minutes and hang the lights."

It's only then that my mom gets off the ladder and practically falls into my father's arms. The relief on her face is clear. "Thank you," she says to him and gives him a kiss. "I don't know what I would do without you."

My dad grins at her like he just won a medal. "Let's hope we don't ever have to find out."

The wedding planner stands there awkwardly,

pretending to be occupied by something written on her clipboard.

When Mom turns to her, the planner says, "Why don't you go start getting ready with the girls? The makeup team is all set up and ready for you. If you'd like, when the tent is finished, I'll let you know, so you can make sure everything is to your satisfaction. Again, I apologize for the error. I hope you will be able to relax and enjoy your time with your daughter from here on out."

"Thank you. I will. And, yes, I would like to see the final product with enough time to make any necessary changes."

She and my dad leave. The tent is empty. My sisters must have gone to the house to get ready, knowing I was going to get our father.

I realize my life is at a turning point. That this weekend is like a pivot. And I have two big decisions to make. The first is easy. I need to heal old wounds. I need to go to the house, talk to my dad, and probably apologize to my mom. Maybe explain the pressure I felt, even though I now know it was probably out of love. I mean, it would be scary as a parent for your child to announce she was moving away. That she wanted a completely different life than the one you'd envisioned for her.

And I hope that will spark them to apologize too. To tell me that they are proud of what I've accomplished. That they understand why I had to do what

I did. And that it was the right decision for me.

But today is not the day. Not on my sister's wedding day.

I'll talk to them about all this tomorrow before I leave town.

Then, there's the next issue.

Carter was going to propose?

Honestly, I can't even deal with that right now.

It's just too much all at once.

Because I think in order to have a future with him, I need to get a handle on my past.

I GO TO the house, pour myself a mimosa, which is very heavy on the champagne, and then proceed to change into one of the matching robes my sister bought everyone to wear for today. We pose for numerous getting-ready shots, and then it's my turn to get my makeup done. It's something I'm used to, and I can practically sleep through the process.

An hour and a half and a whole lot of girlie laughter and fun going on around me later, I'm next up in the chair to get my hair curled and pulled back into a twist.

The wedding planner comes in and gets Mom to go check on everything, and she's happy when she returns.

"Everything looks just perfect, Lakelyn," she says, her eyes sparkling.

And I can tell she's thrilled to have been able to

do all this for her daughter. She and Lakelyn hug tightly, and then Mom presents her with our great-grandmother's pearl earrings to wear for the ceremony.

I'm actually tearing up, and I find myself wishing my mother and I had a better relationship.

ONCE I'M READY, I go upstairs and put on my dress.

I'm just down the stairs and making my way back to the dining room when my dad steps out of his study.

"Can you come in here for a moment?" he asks politely.

I take a fleeting glance toward the dining room, where I can see the girls gathered, sipping mimosas and chatting excitedly.

"Uh, sure. What's up?" I ask with a smile.

"I think it's time you come home."

Oh, for goodness' sake. *Really? He has to start this now?*

"You think so?"

"I do. We'd like to see more of you. We'd like to see you more settled."

"I'm engaged," I say. "I'm getting there, obvious-ly."

"And we really like Carter. But I am good at reading people. Something is off between the two of you. Or with your career. Is it something you'd like to discuss?"

I try to remain calm, but all the old hurt comes out in my voice. "My career, the one you think is stupid, is going quite well actually. I just signed a multimillion-dollar contract to be the face of a very successful designer brand."

"Regardless, you seem unsettled. You don't even own a home. It's no way to live. A person needs grounding. You need a real life."

"The last time I checked, my life is real. *Very* real. And I like it the way it is."

"You have no roots," he scoffs. "Nothing steady."

"You don't have the slightest idea of what I have, *Dad*. I travel all over the world. I have friends all over the world. I make a lot of money. I have people in my life who I care about and who care about me. I've never spent a holiday alone. But you dismiss it all."

He scoffs again, "Carter is a good man. But nothing he's said has indicated that you are willing to settle down. Even though you agreed to marry him. How is your life going to work?"

"We'll figure it out. It's none of your business."

"My children, no matter how old they get or how high-horsed they get, will always be my business," he says. "You need to be here some. With your family. You're missing out on your nieces and nephews growing up." He waves a hand, scowling. "You had your fun. But life isn't about fun. It's about hard work. About building something. You aren't building a legacy, Vale. Once your looks fade and jobs stop coming in, what will you have?"

"How dare you," I whisper. I'm so outraged that I can barely hold back the tears, but there is no way I'm going to let him see me cry because I'm angry. He'll read it as a weakness. "You have *never once* reached out. Never offered to come out and see what *I've* built. The career *I* have. The life *I* live. *Never.* Don't you dare talk to me about my life when you don't have the first clue what it's about."

"I know what I need to know."

"How?!" I shout. "How do you know? No one in this family knows, and you want to know why? Because they're all too afraid of crossing *you*!"

"You could've come home!"

"For what? *This*?!" I throw my hands into the air. "I should've come home, so I could hear the big speech about how my place is in the home?"

His mouth opens like he's about to throw off a comeback, but the door to the study opens.

"What's going on?" Lakelyn says. Her eyes are wide, and her hair is in huge rollers. "I could hear you down the hall."

I have to deliberately compose my face. "Everything's fine. Just the same old argument."

"Dad," she mutters, teeth clenched, "you promised me you wouldn't do this! Not at my wedding!"

"I'm just trying to get her to come home once in a while." He points to me. "She needs to get off her high horse and just listen for once."

"Just like my place is here too, right?" Lakelyn says. When she juts out her chin, she looks downright vicious. "I'm already tired of hearing that from you, so I can only imagine how sick of it Vale must be by now. What is it with you and this obsession with keeping us here? You know AJ and I will be moving around."

"Did it ever occur to you, Dad, that your children might have dreams of their own? Just like you probably did when you were young?"

"It doesn't really matter," Lakelyn says. "Not today anyway. It's my wedding day, and you are both ruining everything!"

"I'm ruining things?" Dad's face goes red. "I'd like to remind you, young lady, of just who's paying for this huge wedding of yours."

"And that's exactly the same as you wanting all of us working for you. To keep us dependent so that you can call the shots," I yell.

"That isn't at all what I'm about, young lady," Dad replies, "and you would know that if you bothered to visit every once in a while."

"Why would I come home for this? So you can remind me why my life isn't good enough for you?"

"Enough. Both of you!" Lakelyn steps between us, her voice shaking with emotion. "Dad, I am so disappointed in you." She turns to me. "And you promised you'd get along. I asked you both for one weekend of peace. Instead, you have turned my wedding into a disaster."

"I've tried to give you everything you dreamed of for your big day," my dad says to Lakelyn, looking stricken.

"I. Didn't. Ask. For. A. Big. Wedding," she says, her teeth clenched. "AJ and I wanted a small destination wedding. *You* and *Mom* wanted this. And you know what? I'm done."

She rushes out of the room in tears, and I hear AJ out in the hall, asking her what's wrong.

The boys must be back from golfing. Dad blusters his way out there, ready for a fight.

"I knew they would fight," Lakelyn sobs, throwing herself into AJ's chest. "It's why I wanted to elope in the first place. I'm sorry, AJ, but I can't marry you today. Not now. Not like this."

"What are you saying?" my father demands.

"It's over, sir," AJ says. He stands up straight and holds my sister tightly. "Lakelyn agreed to this whole weekend because it's what you wanted. And because you promised not to fight with Vale. Now, it's over. The wedding is off. We're going to elope, and you won't get to see your daughter walk down the aisle. Because *you've* ruined what was supposed to be her special day."

"You can't be serious!" my father yells. "Everything is ready! The guests will be arriving soon."

CHAPTER TWENTY
THE EXTRA MILE.

Carter

WHEN I GET back from golfing, I get a text from my sister-in-law.

> **Ashlyn:** I might be with the family, having lunch on the terrace right now.
>
> **Me:** That's great. Tell everyone I said hi.
>
> **Ashlyn:** We might be talking about fate.
>
> **Me:** Oh boy.
>
> **Ashlyn:** Your fate. And I was just wondering, how's that going?

I'm getting ready to text her back when I notice that most of the bridal party as well as the wedding planner and her staff are in front of the barn, all looking concerned.

I walk in their direction.

The wedding planner says to Raine, "So, the wedding is off?"

"It's not off. They are going to elope," Brooke counters.

"I meant, is it off for today? Should we stop setting up?" the wedding planner asks.

Raine turns to Blake. "What do you think?"

"Lakelyn's in tears, and Vale's leaving," Blake says.

"What did I miss? What happened?" I ask, moving toward them.

Lakelyn and AJ couldn't have gotten into a fight. We just got back from golfing.

"Vale and Dad started the same old argument again. Lakelyn got into the mix, and now, everything's a total mess," Blake says with a shrug.

Raine does the same thing.

"Why don't you ever stick up for Vale?" I ask because I don't get it.

"Because they are both stubborn and can't see the forest through the trees," Brooke says. "Dad doesn't really want her to come home forever. He just … it was really hard on him and Mom when she just upped and left. Dad's bitter about it, but he always goes back to the same message. Vale only hears that her family is trying to hold her back. And I don't think that's what Dad means, even back then. I think he was scared of what would happen if she went to LA at eighteen by herself. But she wouldn't hear any of it."

"I can see both sides, even more so now that I have kids," Raine says. "If one of my babies wanted to do what Vale did, I'd be upset too. It would be a fine balance between holding on and letting go. Us siblings, we try to stay neutral, I guess."

"And she said she's leaving?" I ask.

"Yep. Maybe you can talk some sense into her. I'm sure if she and Dad made up, Lakelyn wouldn't be so upset," Brooke says.

Ashlyn: *???*

Me: *Don't ask. It's not. It's a disaster. Fate says I'm an idiot.*

I run to the house, take the stairs two at a time, and go into her bedroom.

She's crying and storming around the room, throwing things into her suitcase. "Call up the jet. Do whatever you have to. Just get me the hell out of here."

"Hang on a second." I take her by the arms and hold her in place. "Tell me what happened."

"What do you think happened? He did what he always does. You know, he had the nerve to tell me it's time to come home and take my place alongside the rest of the family. Like my career, the life I've built, has no value. Can you believe that?"

"Can I believe it? Yes, having recently met him."

To this response, I get a teeny smile. "You know what I mean. And then Lakelyn heard us fighting, and she broke down crying and said he had promised her that he wouldn't fight with me. Apparently, she and AJ wanted a small destination wedding and even considered eloping. But they had it here because it was what our parents wanted. Now, Lakelyn is sad. AJ is pissed. The wedding is off. And I need to get out of here before I lose it, Carter. I really, really do."

I pull her against my chest. She bursts into fresh tears.

"Why does he have to be like that?" she asks, her voice cracking. "I don't need his approval. I really don't. Yet, for some stupid reason, I want it."

"You're strong. Smart. You know what you want and always have. It's one of the things I've always admired about you."

"I wish my father felt that way. To him, I'm not good enough."

"I'm not exactly sure that's what he means."

She stiffens. "Don't you dare try to defend him."

"I'm not trying to defend him. I'm trying to help you feel better. There's a difference."

I smooth the hair back from her face, where tears made it stick. "I'm just curious if you've ever tried to talk about what happened in the past. I agree that he handled it wrong. He should have given you his full support, but—"

"But what?" she fumes.

"Nothing," I say, knowing I need to think about her. But at the same time, I think her reconciling with her father is what would be best for her. And their family.

"I'm sorry I got you involved in this whole

messed up situation, Carter," she sobs.

I raise an eyebrow at her. "But, hey, I learned to bale hay." To this, I get a chuckle. "Do you really think the wedding will be called off?" I glance outside. "Everything looks so beautiful. It would kind of be a shame. What do you say? The sex was amazing last night. Maybe we should get married today instead."

This completely changes her body language from pissed off to slightly amused.

She tilts her head and studies me. "I know you aren't serious, but … somehow, that comment has calmed me down a bit."

"You don't want you and your dad's argument to stop your little sister's wedding. I know, deep down, you don't."

"You're right," she says with a sigh. "I don't. But I don't know how to fix it. And AJ sounded pretty serious."

"Answer me one question. If I could fix things— you know it's what I'm good at, negotiating—would you stay for the wedding? We can leave the second it's over. I'll stand by you the entire night."

"You really are a good guy, Carter," she says. She moves out of my arms and walks over to her window. "It all is really pretty."

"Then, you stay here. Give me a minute. I'm going to find AJ."

"What will you say to AJ?"

"I'm not sure, but regardless of what Lakelyn said earlier, she's been planning to marry the love of her life today. She's going to be upset if it doesn't happen."

She sighs again and plops down in a chair by the window. "You're probably right about that. I knew I shouldn't have come."

"Just … give me a little time. I think I might have an idea on how to work this out."

I FIND AJ out by the barn, talking on his phone. It doesn't take a mind reader to know what's going on with him. The look of rage on his face tells me all I need to know.

"The first flight you can manage. Yes, today. Right away." He's pacing back and forth, his fist all balled up and jammed in his pocket.

"You know," I say, "if you had an agent, you wouldn't have to worry about doing things like this yourself when life goes south."

He looks at me, still on the phone, and shakes his head. His eyes telling me that now's not the time.

But it is the time. Time for this family to heal.

"AJ, I gave you a whole lot of free advice this weekend. Could you just give me a minute?" I ask, hands raised. "Then, you can go back to planning your elopement. In fact, I'll sweeten the deal. You don't need to book a flight. You can take my plane to wherever you want to go."

"Are you trying to bribe me?"

"It's pretty obvious all you want to do is make Lakelyn happy. I respect that. The offer is there because I feel bad that your wedding plans fell apart."

"Fine." He hangs up his phone and slides it into his pocket.

"In your heart, do you really think Lakelyn wants to walk away from all this?" I indicate everything with a sweep of an arm. All the planning. All the decor. All her dreams.

"I don't know. In the moment? When she's crying hysterically and pissed off at her dad? Yeah, she wants to flip him off with both hands and drive the hell away." He lets out a sigh. "Later though? I think she might regret it. We're here, and it's hours before the wedding. We have guests coming. People have traveled here just for the wedding. And it will break her mother's heart."

"She'll feel bad about it."

He nods. "Eventually, I think so. She won't want to hear that right now though."

"Understood. Do me a favor. Bring her out on the front porch in about ten minutes. Tell her there's something she'll want to see."

"What is it?"

"I'm not completely sure yet," I admit, "but I think it'll make her happy. Maybe make the whole family happy."

As I'm jogging back toward the house, he calls

out, "Why are you going to all this trouble?"

"Didn't I already tell you? This is what I do. I go the extra mile!"

I GO INTO the house and talk Vale into coming outside.

"Why are we out here?" she asks. Everything about her body language screams how upset she is. She has her arms wrapped around herself and her shoulders hunched.

"Do you trust me?" I take her chin and tip her head upward, so she can look me in the eye.

"I don't know. I still don't understand why you said what you did when I called after the new year. Why you didn't confront me that night and let me explain."

"I was hurt," I tell her. "Just like you are now. And I said some things I regret. How about we handle one problem at a time?"

"What are you two doing out here?" Mr. Martin's voice rings out. "I figured you'd have hit the road by now."

"Is this why you brought me out here?" Vale hisses at me. "I take it back. I don't trust you."

"Vale, there's something between you and your father that's gone unsaid for too long."

"What would that be? He's never exactly held back his opinions. No matter how much they hurt me."

I look toward her dad and say, "If you don't tell her, I will."

"What are you talking about?" he asks.

"Tell her how you really feel. Tell her about the book," I urge.

He glances away, but I march straight up to him and get in his face. "Tell her about it. Now. Or you're going to lose half your family today. And those who don't leave will lose all respect for you. You're in what I would call a lose-lose situation here. Swallow your pride and tell her the truth."

"What book?" Vale asks out of curiosity, but then she crosses her arms again. "Honestly, it doesn't matter. Being out here is pointless, Carter. Nothing is going to change. My father will always hate me."

Mr. Martin winces, and I know she's hurt him. I know he doesn't hate her. And it kills him for her to think that he does. I definitely know now where Vale got her stubbornness from.

"Tell her about the book," I say one more time. "You'll be glad you did."

His mouth moves, but nothing comes out.

Which leaves me no choice. "Vale, your father has kept a scrapbook with pictures of probably every modeling job you've ever done. It's in his study. I know he's proud of you even if he won't admit it."

I'm a little worried that Mr. Martin might kill me, but the look on Vale's face makes whatever consequences there might be totally worth it.

It's like watching the dawn break over the horizon after a long, stormy night.

ALL THIS TIME.

Carter

"DAD? IS THAT true? You've kept a book?" she asks him in disbelief.

"Well, yeah. It's nothing big. Some clippings from some of your jobs, is all." He takes off his hat, smacking it against his thigh.

"It is a big deal, Vale," I counter. "It's years' worth of photos. *All* of them."

"Why did you do that?" she whispers to her dad.

"Well …"

"I thought you hated what I did. I thought you were ashamed of me. I thought you'd tried to forget about me."

"I might've said a lot of things I wish I hadn't," he answers sincerely.

"So, you don't hate what I do?" Vale asks.

"I hate that you left home, Vale. That's what I have always hated. But as for being ashamed of you?" He shakes his head. "Never. You forged your own path. You're successful. I'm proud of what you have accomplished."

She can't hold back the tears. "How? Why? When did you change your mind about all this?"

He lets out a long sigh. One he's probably been holding back for some time. And hopefully a cleansing one.

"You'll understand someday, maybe, when you have children of your own," he says. "You say and do things for their own good because you want to protect them. I worked hard all these years, building something, but I didn't do it for me. I did it for you all because I wanted you to be taken care of. I didn't want you to have to work as hard as I had to. There were a lot of lean years there in the beginning. I wanted better than that for you." He looks up at the sky, the way a man does when there's something on his face he doesn't want anyone to see. "And then you just turned your back on it. On me. On your family. You didn't want what I had worked hard to give you. It felt like a slap in the face."

"That's not how it was from my perspective, Dad. Do you want to know how hard it was for me? How I felt?"

He nods. And I'm slightly relieved.

I was hoping they might hug and make up at this point, but Vale isn't done with him yet. Probably from the hurt she's held in for so long.

"You try to control everything. You wanted to control how I lived my life. What I did. Where I worked. Even now, my coming home after all these years, all you can say to me is that I need to come home and settle down. Would you want anyone, even *your* father, ordering you around? Telling what you *have* to do? Especially when you know that person has no idea what you want. Mostly because he won't freaking listen to you."

"I do know actually," Mr. Martin states.

"What do you mean?" Vale asks.

"I know what it feels like to have your old man boss you around." He lets out a seemingly surprised chuckle.

"I can't believe you think this is funny," she says, getting pissed again.

"I'm not laughing at you. I'm laughing at me because I'm an idiot. I just realized that I put you through what my dad had put me through. He wanted me to stay on the farm. Wanted me to continue running it. To not expand our holdings. He thought it meant the farm wasn't good enough for me. That he wasn't good enough."

"Was that how you felt?" she asks.

"Of course not. I respected him. I just … wanted to build something of my own. And I did."

"I wanted something of my own too. And I got it, Dad. Just like you did. I love my life. My career. I don't need you to be happy about it, but I do need you to respect it. And when you said what you did, it hurt. Still, after all this time."

"I didn't mean to hurt you. I never mean to hurt you," he says, getting misty-eyed.

When he holds out his arms to her, she walks straight into them. And even though we've been here for a couple of days, I feel like she's just finally come home.

I don't want to interrupt, but at the same time, we have another pressing matter, so I clear my throat and ask the million-dollar question, "Does this mean you're planning on staying for the wedding, Vale?"

"Of course." She brushes away her tears. "I have to go apologize to Lakelyn for causing all this drama."

"No need," Lakelyn says. "AJ insisted I come out here but wouldn't tell me why. I figured I could give Dad a piece of my mind, if nothing else."

"Oh? You think I need a piece of your mind?" He raises a bushy eyebrow at Lakelyn.

"Since it sometimes seems like you've both lost yours? Yeah," she fires back. But she gives both Vale and her father a grin before throwing her arms around them.

"We cool?" Vale asks her.

"We're cool." Lakelyn grins back. "And if it's okay with you all, I'd really like to marry AJ today."

CHAPTER TWENTY-ONE
BLINK OF AN EYE.

Carter

EVERYTHING FROM THAT point on moves quickly. Soon, we're all showered, shaved, and dressed. The photographer takes a few shots of the groom and his groomsmen before we head down to where we're to begin the wedding processional.

I line up next to Vale's grandma, who studies me closely.

"That isn't Trent's suit. You don't have the same body type, but it's tailored to perfection. How did they manage to get one so quickly?" Grandma asks, looking me up and down.

"I was lucky I brought a black suit with me. You look lovely, by the way. Your dress is beautiful."

"Sweet-talker," she says with a smirk, but she clearly loves it.

I escort her down the aisle and then take my place in the gazebo next to AJ.

I hear Jake gulp as he waves his daughter down the aisle.

I can understand why he's worried. I can't forget the image of her dolls flying out of the wagon.

As it turns out, there was nothing to fear. Sophie does a repeat of her performance for me last night. Her head is held high, and she walks slowly, so everyone can admire her dress.

By the time she's finished, her happy smile has turned to consternation.

She lets go of the wagon handle and marches toward me. "Say I look beautiful," she demands.

"The flower girl looks so lovely," I stage whisper with astonishment, just like I did when she was practicing. "What a beautiful dress. I'm so glad she walked slow enough so that I could see it. And her shoes just sparkle."

She gives me a practically regal head nod as I notice the bridal party holding back their laughter. The kid just totally stole the show.

But then Vale walks through the wooden doors. I didn't see her before when we lined up. She stayed with Lakelyn, who didn't want AJ to see her in her dress until she walked down the aisle.

The bridesmaids are all wearing flowing dresses in a soft pink, but Vale's dress is different. It's a dark rose color, and it's more fitted, showing off her gorgeous figure.

I've seen her on catwalks. I've watched her stroll confidently into parties and high-profile events. I've seen her lying in my bed the morning after. But I've never seen her look quite as beautiful as she does right now. Or honestly, as happy.

And when she looks straight into my eyes, I swear, just like the first time we met, I forget how to breathe.

COULD HAVE BEEN US.

Vale

I'M HAPPY THAT I'm here. Happy I'm home. Happy my father and I came to some sort of an agreement.

But when Carter's eyes meet mine as I step into the gazebo, I feel even happier.

And I can't help but think, *This could have been us.*

It's funny how, sometimes, you get in your own way.

I realize that I am quick to react. I reacted poorly when my dad tried to talk to me about going to LA. When I wouldn't listen to anything he said because my mind was made up, he got defensive. Hurt even. Which made me get that whole *I'll show you* attitude.

I did the same thing to Carter in a way. I was mad when he told me he wasn't sure he'd make it to my party. Hurt even. And I kissed someone else instead. To prove a point somehow. Another *I'll show you* moment.

I didn't want to kiss that guy. I wanted to be kissing Carter. And I should have told him how I felt about it. I should have told him that I loved him.

How I think he's the most perfect man I've ever met. Well, maybe not perfect. But perfect for me.

I think about the misconceptions I had about my mother's life. About my parents' relationship. I saw what I wanted to see.

He holds my gaze, his eyes speaking to me in a way that indicates he feels the same way.

I just don't know where we go from here.

And part of me is afraid to try. Afraid to consider the fact that he actually wanted to marry me. That he was going to propose. And that I would have said yes.

Because deep down, I do want to share my life with him. I just don't want to lose myself in the process. And if I didn't know it before this weekend, I certainly know now that Carter Crawford is a really, really good man.

Maybe too good for me.

When the wedding march starts playing and the doors open again, he breaks our gaze, turning his head away.

The second I see Lakelyn and my father together, tears spring to my eyes. Her dress is perfect for her. A beautiful creamy lace dress covered in rhinestones over a pale pink underlay. She has a crown of flowers on her head and a long veil draping down her back. But it's the absolute joy radiating from her face that gets me the most. And the way she looks at AJ, like he's the only person in the room.

AJ is struggling to hold back his emotion and not winning. He might be a beast on the football field, but he's a big softy when it comes to my sister.

And it's that sort of love. That kind of adoration. That I want.

I want to know what it feels like to have my father give me away to the man I love. I want to watch emotion wash over his face when he sees me.

I just have to figure out how to have that and not lose myself in the process.

SO MUCH LOVE.

Carter

AJ AND LAKELYN have written their own vows, combining traditional ones with their own words of love.

I know they are just words. The kind that couples have been repeating to others for centuries.

There is so much love in them. So much hope.

Lakelyn's eyes shine with tears, but she hasn't stopped smiling yet. Not even for a second.

I've watched my siblings, my clients, and my friends get married. But it wasn't until Vale walked toward me, even only as a bridesmaid, that I finally grasped the utter magnitude of the moment.

Because when the right girl is walking toward you, wearing a wedding dress, you know that your life, your future, is wrapped up in her.

It's hard to keep my thoughts from wandering toward what I wanted. What I envisioned. Especially with Vale standing across from me with my ring on her finger.

"You may now kiss the bride," the officiant says.

When AJ bends down to kiss Lakelyn, their guests clap and cheer.

"Time to party!" Blake announces, earning him a laugh from those around him.

We wait until Lakelyn and AJ are down the aisle before meeting in front of the minister. Vale takes my arm.

"You're beautiful," I murmur, lifting her hand to my lips and kissing it before tucking it in the crook of my arm.

"And you're the hero," she whispers. "This wouldn't have happened if it wasn't for you."

"I don't know about that."

We start down the aisle, smiling for the photographer.

"I do. This could've ended in disaster, but you brought us back together."

Once we're at the end of the aisle, we stop and turn to each other.

"You have a good family. Tough. Complicated. But they're good people, and they love you." *And so do I*, I want to add, but I can't bring myself to do it. There's still that last scrap of pride holding me back.

She kisses me softly, tenderly, and leaves behind an ache in my heart.

CHAPTER TWENTY-TWO
WRONG ABOUT HIM.

Vale

"CAN I HAVE this dance?"

I turn away from the bar to find my father holding his hand out to me. He looks dashing in his tuxedo—a far cry from his usual chambray shirt and jeans.

Funny. Before this afternoon, I would've accepted his invitation for appearances only.

Now, I'm actually happy he's leading me out onto the dance floor.

"It's turned out to be a beautiful wedding. A beautiful day," I say, looking around us.

All the guests are having a great time—laughing, dancing, eating, drinking. Love is most definitely in the air.

"And I nearly ruined it," Dad says.

"We both lost our tempers. On more than one occasion over the years."

"You know I'm not a man who shares his feelings easily. I'm not one of these, you know, touchy-feely men. But I still should have been upfront with you. I should have told you how it made me feel when you were so determined to leave. It wasn't until you brought up my father today that I really understood." He pauses for a moment before continuing, "Having you back for a couple of days isn't good enough. As soon as you showed up, everything felt right again. I didn't know until you got here that something had been missing. Sure, I missed you. I know your mother missed you. But actually having you here? Now I know how much it hurts when you're gone."

"Oh, Daddy." I brush away a tear.

"I suppose today was my last-ditch attempt at trying to get you to stay. You'll find as kids grow up and get minds of their own, you get tired of arguing and reasoning with them. And at some point, you snap and realize you sound like a parent. I should have told you my concerns." He is silent for a moment. "And sometimes, it's a lot easier to be mad than, uh, sort through your feelings."

"I'm pretty sure you passed that trait on to me." I let out a chuckle and then get serious again. "I think you should be a little more attuned to Mom's needs."

"Vale," he says, his eyes big and his face looking downright scandalized.

"Ohmigawd, Dad. That's *not at all* what I meant. I just meant, do you make her feel valued? Is she happy?"

"I think you might have misjudged your mother. Just because her life isn't what you imagined yours to be like doesn't mean she's not happy. I know you think I'm the one who controls things but not when it comes to her. I have a lot of bravado, sure, but your mother has always ruled the roost. And I'd do anything to keep her happy. Mostly. The only time I didn't was when it had to do with you. But when you never came back and never even called, it hurt her a lot. She understands when you love stubborn people like us, you have to let them do their own thing—even if you disagree with how they do it." His hand tightens around mine. "If you didn't understand earlier today, I want you to know now, Vale. I was afraid if you didn't have your mother and me to rely on, you'd lose yourself in the world. I should have known better. You've always been the strongest-willed of all our kids. And I am very proud of the woman you've become."

"If you had said that when I got here, the weekend would have been a lot more fun," I say with a chuckle.

He nods toward the corner of the dance floor, where Sophie is happily monopolizing Carter's attention. And the sight of her sparkly pink shoes on top of his so they can dance together is enough to make my heart ache.

"I like him a lot," he says.

And suddenly, it all feels like too much.

Being here with Carter. Feeling the way I do about him. Hearing my father praise my fake fiancé.

I excuse myself, pretending to need the bathroom, but what I really need is a moment to myself.

Or else today's meltdown won't be the last time one of us Martin girls is in tears.

ALWAYS BEEN YOURS.

Carter

SOPHIE STICKS OUT her bottom lip. "I wanna dance with you again."

"Actually"—I crouch down, so we're face-to-face—"I was hoping I could dance with your aunt Vale."

"Come on, you." Brooke picks up her daughter, balancing her on one hip. "You've taken up enough of Carter's time."

"I loved every minute of it." I wink at Sophie, who manages a tiny smile in the midst of her disappointment.

But I need to go find Vale.

The girl who has my heart.

I search the dance floor but don't find her, so I step outside the tent.

"Hey, if you're looking for my sister," Blake says, "she's down in the gazebo, talking to Trent."

"Trent? Is he well enough to be here?"

"Apparently. He wanted to talk to her before she left town."

I make my way past the barn, needing to know what's happening out there.

I enter the gardens, and as I'm going down the main path, I find Trent being pushed in a wheelchair. By whom I assume is his mother.

"Hey," I say to him. "How are you feeling?"

"Still pretty sore, but I wanted to at least come and congratulate AJ and Lakelyn."

"That's nice of you. Are they in the gazebo?" I ask even though I know they are not.

"No, I was chatting with Vale. I heard she and her father made amends. I figured it was time we did the same. Put the past behind us."

And my heart goes out to him again. I know that girl isn't easy to forget.

"Did it go okay?"

He nods. "Yeah, I think so. I'll see you later."

His mother continues their trek to the barn, and I move farther toward my destination. Toward her.

I find her sitting on the railing of the gazebo, dangling her feet over the edge, swinging them back and forth.

I wish I could get a picture of her right now. I wish there were a camera in existence that could capture her beauty. Sitting there, surrounded by the glow of flickering lanterns. Her hair swept up, her face tilted back so she can look at the stars. And I can't help but wonder what she's thinking about.

When she looks down at the ring on her left hand—my ring—I know.

"This seat taken?" I ask her.

"Of course not. Sit. Sorry, you startled me. I was so deep in thought that I didn't hear you coming."

"I saw Trent. Looks like he's on the mend."

"Physically, yes. And hopefully emotionally too. I hurt a lot of people when I just upped and left."

"We haven't really gotten to talk about New Year's Eve. I think I need to tell you everything." I pick up her hand. "Obviously, this is the ring I had designed for you. The ring I had in my pocket the night I was going to propose. My flight was delayed due to weather. Traffic was horrible. I made it there just before midnight. When I found you, the ball hadn't dropped yet. But there you were, kissing another man. After that, proposing really didn't seem appropriate."

"Why didn't you confront me? Or tell me when I called you a few days after? If it were me, I would have been pissed and wanted you to know it."

"Because I felt like nothing you could say would matter. That you had already given me your answer."

"But you kept the ring?"

"Kind of had to. It was custom. Eventually, I'll

have it stripped apart to sell the diamonds, but"—I lower my head, my voice tightening—"I just haven't yet." I let out a sardonic chuckle. "And now, we know why. So we could pretend to be engaged."

"Is that what you want?" she asks.

"To pretend to be engaged?"

"Yes."

"No. It's not what I want. I've wanted you to be mine since the night we met. But you seemed … elusive. So, I just let you do your thing. I was afraid I would push you away if I acted too serious. Chloe set me straight about that."

"She did?"

"She told me to stop asking the coach to put me in if he feels like it. You're the coach in this scenario."

"I figured."

"It made me realize that was how I treated us. I was so glad to be with you whenever you wanted to be with me that I didn't want to rock the boat by coming out and saying I wanted more."

She sighs. "So long as we're being honest … I don't know how I would've reacted then. If you had proposed. I mean, I would've been swept up by it, and had I accepted, I would've meant it. But …"

"You would've had second thoughts."

"I had—have issues to process. Baggage to unpack. It's all so mixed up." She shakes her head, and I notice her hand trembling in mine. "*I'm* all so mixed up."

"We're older than AJ and Lakelyn. We've got separate careers and lives, and for us to work, we'd have to figure out how to combine them. I'm not telling you what happened to make you feel guilty or to pressure you in any way. I simply want you to know how I feel. It's why I couldn't give up the ring."

The DJ in the wedding tent plays a sweet, slow song, the sound drifting toward us.

"Can I have this dance? I'm pretty sure it's tradition for the maid of honor and the best man to have at least one dance."

She rolls her eyes but laughs. "Can't break tradition, can we?"

WE DANCE SLOWLY and then make our way back to the reception tent. We don't want to miss the cutting of the cake.

No sooner are we on the dance floor and back in each other's arms than AJ breaks through the crowd with his father.

"I'm convinced," Mr. Barnett says.

I met him when we were getting ready for the wedding today, but we haven't spoken a word about anything else.

"Convinced?" I look at AJ for answers.

"That I should sign with you," AJ explains with a grin. "Dad talked to Mr. Martin, and everyone is in agreement."

I shake his dad's hand. "It will be a pleasure representing your son, Mr. Barnett." Then, I turn to AJ. "We're going to have to hustle to get everything ready for the draft. When do you leave for your honeymoon?"

"We want to get settled in our new city first."

"Thank goodness. I wouldn't have wanted to go on your honeymoon with you," I tease.

"Congratulations," Vale murmurs.

I'm not sure if she's talking to me or to the Barnetts. I just know she slips away while AJ's dad hammers me with questions.

Strange how I feel like I lost an opportunity, even while in the midst of gaining a client. I should be happy, but I'm not.

I want more. I want her.

CHAPTER TWENTY-THREE
FAIRY-TALE LIFE.

Carter

WE DON'T TALK further about our relationship. About the past or the future the rest of the night. We just enjoy dancing and having fun at the wedding.

When the last guest has left, we make our way up to her bedroom.

And it just happens.

Slowly peeling her clothes off, one piece at a time. Lowering her to the bed so I can worship every inch of her body. Taking my time with her.

She falls forward, her hair like a waterfall all around me, covering my mouth with hers and moaning into it.

There's something between us tonight that has never been there before.

And I'm not sure I like it because it feels like she's saying good-bye to me.

Like it's our last time.

When she moves off me, she closes her eyes and is quiet.

I think she's gone to sleep, but then she rolls over and whispers, "I didn't think you wanted a relationship, Carter. I'd heard about you and your brothers—players on and off the field."

"And I heard you were dating some rich guy while you were dating me. Were you in love with him?" I ask, wanting the truth.

"No," she says, shaking her head. "We met at a resort where I was doing a shoot, and it started off innocently enough with a drink. He said I made him feel crazy and asked if I would fly with him to Paris in his private plane. After checking with my agent, who confirmed that he was who he'd said he was and not like a serial killer, I said yes. He had a pied-à-terre overlooking the Eiffel Tower, and it was so luxurious. He took me on a shopping spree, bought me a diamond necklace. I got caught up in it. When I say it now, I feel so dumb, but even though I've earned a lot of money, I've saved most of it because I'm just some girl from Iowa who an agent happened to see in a local swimsuit ad. Next thing I knew, I was in catalogs, designer ads, and on magazine covers. Even so, his lifestyle seemed so over the top, you know?"

"So, you want a rich guy?"

"I can take care of myself, so it wasn't about the money. It was more that it all seemed … well, like a fairy tale."

"Is that what you want?"

"All I've ever known is what I don't want."

"What's that?"

"No white picket fences. No kids. No going home to live on the family farm."

"What's wrong with kids and the farm? I've actually had a pretty good time here."

"Well, until this weekend, I would have said everything. But being here with my sisters and Blake. Even my parents. I see things in a new light." She smirks. "And they love you."

"I'm a lovable guy," I joke. "Trustworthy, loyal, dedicated to bringing families together in times of crises."

"I know you're only kidding, but there's a lot of truth to what you're saying."

I reach over and gently brush a strand of hair off of her face. "You want to hear about loyalty? How serious I've been about us all this time? I didn't date or sleep with anyone else during the time we seemed like we were getting closer. Or since my failed New Year's Eve proposal."

"Really?" she asks.

"Really. And I have some advice for you. If you want a fairy-tale life, choose a guy you love because of who he is—his morals, ethics, values, and the butterflies he puts in your stomach whenever he's around. I was in love with you when I planned to propose and still am, but I've never been second string, Vale. And I won't be yours. So, while I'd love to see you when we get back home, I'm done being your booty call. I want more."

And I find this ironic because I have been on the receiving end of this kind of ultimatum before.

"Like, you want to date or something?"

"No, Vale, I want to marry you. I also really want kids. So, that might be a deal-breaker for us."

She sighs. "I want kids too. I just—"

"I get it. Your relationship with your family has been complicated."

"And I haven't had a chance to sort all my feelings out."

"You have time." I take her chin, gently moving her head so she's looking me in the eye. "Not forever though. I'm not going to pressure you. I know what I want, and I can't live in between. I'm serious about this. About us. So, go home. Think about it. Sort those feelings out. And let me know."

"Okay," she whispers.

"I think you need to figure out what you want rather than what you don't want."

WON'T BREATHE A WORD.

Vale

IT'S BARELY DAWN when I tiptoe down the stairs. After agreeing to sign with Carter last night, AJ is determined to fly back to LA with us. Lakelyn has to get back to school and study for finals. I was told we'd be leaving early.

Not this early, but before-noon early.

As expected, I find my mother in the kitchen, humming to herself as she prepares breakfast. It'll be another full kitchen this morning.

"How do you do it all?" I ask her.

She jumps, startled, and laughs softly when she finds me standing in the doorway. "Do what, honey? There's coffee if you want it."

Want it? It's a necessity at this point. I'm exhausted even though I couldn't sleep.

"How do you throw parties three nights in a row and then get up before dawn to make sure everyone's fed? I need three days in bed just to recover from last night, and I didn't really do anything."

She chuckles. "I don't know. It's what I do. I wouldn't want life any other way."

I take a seat at the island and help her cut up some fruit. "You really mean that?"

"Of course I do. Honey, it's days like yesterday

that make everything worth it. All the working and the saving, the trials of raising kids—yes, it can be hard," she adds when my eyes go wide.

"Are you happy?"

"Is that what this is about?" She turns to me, mixing bowl under one arm. "Yes, I'm happy. If I wasn't happy, something would need to change. I like things the way they are. Having a full house with your sisters and brother and the babies nearby. It fills me up inside, being surrounded by people I love."

I can't help but feel a little guilty. I'm not a part of that anymore.

"And now that you're settling down, I hope you come out to visit more often. I've missed you. Things don't feel the same without you here."

"Daddy said the same thing," I admit, looking down at the strawberries I'm cutting the tops off of, avoiding her eyes.

"Well then, you know it must be true. He's not big on showing emotion."

"How do you two manage staying together? You're so different."

"We balance each other out, I suppose. Like you and Carter. He's so even-keeled."

I can't take it anymore. I lay the knife on the cutting board and cover my face with my hands. "Oh, Mom. It's all so messed up."

She has me in a hug before I can draw another breath. "Honey, what's the matter? Did you have a fight?"

"We're not really engaged," I blurt out.

She sucks in a breath but doesn't let go of me. If anything, she squeezes tighter.

And that unconditional love makes it all fall out of my mouth at once. How I held him at arm's length, how he planned to propose. "This is the ring he had made for me. He was going to ask me to marry him, but I was already upset because I thought he'd stood me up. I would've said yes, but you know—and this is the worst part—I probably would've changed my mind."

"If you love him and want to marry him, why would you do that?"

"Because I don't know what I actually want. Only what I don't want—or thought I didn't want. That's why everything's such a mess because I don't know anything anymore. This weekend flipped my perceptions on a lot of things."

"Vale, honey, why did you pretend to be engaged?"

I pull away, brushing my hair off my face. "Because I knew you'd try to set me up with Trent. And Daddy did just what I had known he would do. Told me it was time to come home. I figured I'd avoid all that if I was already engaged."

"You should know your father better than that by now."

"Please, don't tell him about this," I beg. "I'm

serious. You're the only person who can know."

"I won't breathe a word of it. You can trust me." She tucks my hair behind my ears with a sigh. "I don't think you give yourself enough credit."

"What do you mean?"

"I mean, you've always known exactly what you want."

"See, that's the thing. I haven't. I've only known what I don't want. Is there something broken in me?"

"No, my beauty. You're perfect the way you are." She pulls me in for another hug. "Now, wash your face before anyone else comes down and finds you crying. And stop being so hard on yourself."

Before she lets go though, she hits me with one of those patented Mom looks. "Do you love him?"

"I do. That much I know. But that isn't enough, or everyone who ever fell in love would get married right away. I don't know if we want the same things. Part of me wonders if I'm even good enough for him. You've seen him in action this weekend. He's incredible."

There's movement on the stairs. I hurry over to the sink to wash my face.

"Good morning." Lakelyn looks a little dazed, a little sleepy, but extremely happy when she joins us. "What's for breakfast?"

If only all of life's questions were so easily answered.

CHAPTER TWENTY-FOUR
A HUGE CRUSH.

Carter

WE SAID OUR good-byes to Vale's family on Sunday, and then AJ, Vale, and I flew back to LA.

I tried to get her to keep the ring, but she insisted on giving it back. She said she wanted to think about everything without the pressure. Without having to sit and stare at it.

But I have a sneaking suspicion the real reason she gave it back. Because she wants a real proposal. Not one we made up.

And she deserves it.

Although she wants to think about what her life will look like if we are together, I don't have to do that. I already know I want to be with her. To love her. For a very long time. And I hope that she will come to the same conclusion.

Fortunately for me, I haven't had much time to sit around and ponder life. It's been a crazy week and a half. Signing AJ. The big announcement. Talking to companies about possible endorsements. Talking to all the teams about him. Going over more than just his stats, like what he brings to the team from a leadership standpoint. You'd think you would only have to focus on the teams with the first few picks in the draft, but you never know when a team is going to trade up for a pick.

AJ flashes a smile from his side of my desk. "This all feels so surreal. I can't believe I got married and left my bride the next day to come out here. It's been a whirlwind."

"You're lucky you graduated in December. Otherwise, you'd be trying to study for finals in the midst of this."

"I'll be honest, I'm getting a little nervous. Not so much about when I get drafted or where, but being on TV. I know I told you I took acting classes when I was young, but this is different. I won't be acting. This is my real life. My future."

"Lakelyn and I will be right by your side the opening night of the draft," I say with a grin, "as will your parents."

"You're right," he says, taking a deep breath.

"But just in case you're still freaking out, I have a little surprise for you today."

His eyes get big, like he can't take much more uncertainty right now. "What kind of surprise?" he asks tentatively.

"While I do my job and talk you up all day, you're going to hang out with my brothers and their wives—Cade and Palmer, Cash and Ashlyn—and a few other special guests. Some friends of ours."

"What kind of friends?"

"Well, let's see. Palmer's brother is Pike Montlake."

"Holy shit," he says.

"Yep. And Palmer, you might know, was on a TV series with Ashlyn and Jennifer Edwards—"

"Who is married to Danny Diamond!"

"And who happens to be in town. Also in attendance will be Harper and Maddox Harper."

"I'm speechless. Really, Carter."

"All these guys have been exactly where you are now. Other than Danny, who got drafted as predicted, the others went off plan simply because the teams keep what they want close to the vest. It's all part of the teams' draft strategies."

My intercom buzzes, and my assistant says, "Ashlyn is here to see you now."

"Oh jeez. Ashlyn Roberts? Take a deep breath, AJ," he says to himself. "I had a huge crush on her, growing up."

Ashlyn breezes in. "So?" she says. "Does fate still say you're an idiot?"

"Probably," I say with a sigh.

I haven't heard from Vale since I dropped her off at her place and she told me she needed time. When I asked how much, she said she needed some space and would call me when she was ready to talk. Then she took off the ring and gave it back to me.

Not wanting to be ambivalent while still respecting her wishes, I sent a gorgeous bouquet of flowers, just signed with my name.

And although the florist said they handed them directly to her, she hasn't said a word to me.

If it wasn't for AJ sitting in my office, I might almost believe I'd dreamed the whole wedding weekend.

"Ash, this is AJ Barnett. AJ, meet Ashlyn. And please, try to take it easy on him," I warn.

"Ah, come on, Carter. You know we will. I mean, we will probably drill him about his, uh, recent nuptials. About certain members of his family."

I roll my eyes as she pats AJ's forearm.

"Come on, big guy. Let's get you ready for the draft."

She turns back to me. "Question."

"Yes?"

"What's he wearing?"

"We haven't gotten that far yet."

"Perfect. I have to stop to pick up a dress on our way home. Why don't you let me get him all fixed up?"

"I didn't even stop to think about what I'd wear. I don't want anything flashy, like some guys wear. It's just not me, and I'd get a truckload of shit about it from my family."

Ashlyn sizes him up and looks at me. "I'm thinking a well-tailored suit, navy blue. A fun tie. Tennis shoes?"

"No way," AJ says. "Not with a suit."

"I like your style. Dress shoes it is. Plus, that will give us time to talk."

What did I get myself into?

"Uh, look, I don't have time to tell the family this, so you're going to have to do it. AJ, Ash, take a seat real quick."

"What's up?" Ashlyn says.

I sit back down in my chair, hands clasped behind my neck. "I'm sorry in advance for what I'm about to tell you both. I don't normally lie, but—"

AJ smirks at me. "You finally gonna fess up that you and Vale weren't really engaged at my wedding? That you only pretended to be, so her dad wouldn't be so hard on her? I knew you had planned to propose to her on New Year's Eve, but that when you got there, she was kissing someone else, and you left. And I know that when she called you a few days later, you told her you weren't interested in her anymore. I also know that neither one of you has gotten over it."

I rock back so hard that it almost tips the chair over.

"I don't understand," I say to AJ. "You knew?"

"I know now," he corrects, taking a seat. "Lakelyn overheard Vale tell their mom about the fake engagement the morning after the wedding." He looks sheepish, slightly embarrassed. "I knew the part about what had happened on New Year's Eve. We sort of pieced it all together. We didn't know your family didn't know though. Sorry."

"Mrs. Martin did give me an extra-tight hug when we left now that I think about it," I say.

"We won't tell anyone," AJ assures me.

"Speak for yourself," Ashlyn says. "I can't keep secrets from the family."

I roll my eyes.

AJ looks at Ashlyn conspiratorially and says to her, "Vale also said she loves Carter and wants to marry him. But that she doesn't know how to combine their lives."

"Sounds like she needs some convincing," Ashlyn says with a big grin.

I tent my fingers under my chin, thinking. "It sounds like I need to explain a few things to the Martins first."

"Getting her father's blessing before you propose again would be a big gesture. What a happy coincidence that we'll be stopping in Iowa on our way to the draft to pick up Lakelyn. Maybe you could carve out some time to visit a certain farm."

Ashlyn narrows her eyes at me. "We need in on this too. Come on, AJ. Let's go get you all gussied up for the draft. You can talk sports with the boys, and then we can plan out Carter's life for him."

This causes AJ to laugh. "I thought I was going to be all starstruck over you. But you're funny. Let's go."

"Look, I've got some calls to make. I'll touch base with you later."

The second they leave, I call my parents.

CHAPTER TWENTY-FIVE
BACK ON A PLANE.

Carter

THE PROFESSIONAL DRAFT in New York City was an exciting event, as always.

Ashlyn had AJ and Lakelyn both dressed appropriately, and our stop in Iowa went well.

AJ ended up going to LA when they traded with Atlanta to get him for the fourth pick overall.

Lakelyn is thrilled, knowing she'll be living near her sister, and AJ, Ashlyn, and Cash have become fast friends.

Which brings me to where I am now.

Back on a plane.

This time with most of my family.

They are raucous and excited, but I'm just a nervous wreck.

CHAPTER TWENTY-SIX
GIRL'S ONLY.

Vale

IT'S SATURDAY, AND I'm having a lazy morning. I got up, got ready, got coffee, and then came back to the house I'm leasing to figure out my plans for today. High on the list is spending the day at the beach.

Possibly a specific beach, where a certain Crawford brother lives.

I think it's about time I give him my answer.

I'm throwing a towel and a few essentials in a bag. If things go the way I hope they do with Carter, I won't be coming home tonight.

Although I should probably call him and not just show up.

But at the same time, if fate wants me to tell him today, he'll be there.

The doorbell rings, and I open my front door to find my little sister and Ashlyn Roberts standing there.

"What are you doing here?" I ask them.

"Did you really not watch the draft?" Lakelyn says.

"Oh no," I reply, feeling bad. "I've been busy with work and all. Did it go well?"

"Hell yeah!" Ashlyn says, throwing her arm around Lakelyn. "We get her here in LA with us!"

"Wait a minute. How do you two know each other?" I ask.

"Oh, I can answer that," Ashlyn says, holding up her hand like she's a student in class. "AJ was nervous about the actual draft process itself. You know, going to the Big Apple. Being on television. Trying to not look disappointed if he didn't get chosen at a certain spot, to a certain team, that kind of thing. So, Carter set up a little get-together with me and Cash, Palmer and Cade, Harper and Maddox, and Jennifer and Danny Diamond. We all got along famously. Oh, and I also helped him pick out the suit he wore to the draft, and he helped me pick out a dress for Lakelyn to wear. Show her, Lake."

Lakelyn pulls out her phone and flashes a photo of her and AJ. They are such a handsome couple. And Ashlyn did good. AJ's suit is tailored to perfectly fit his large frame, and Lakelyn looks stunning.

"Do you think we could come in?" my sister finally asks.

"Sorry. I, well, you surprised me, is all. Of course. I'm sorry the place is kind of messy. The cleaners don't come until tomorrow, and I still haven't unpacked."

"Are you filming?" Ashlyn asks.

"Not for two more weeks," I tell her. "Just photo shoots for the role right now. A few other jobs. Trying to get everything done before all that starts."

"So, you've been busy," Lakelyn observes.

"Uh, yep," I say even though it's not really true.

I have been working but not as much as I'm making it sound like. I've been practicing controlled breathing, doing yoga, working, and then coming home, cooking dinner for myself, and doing some soul-searching. Trying to make thoughtful decisions about my life.

Carter hasn't called. Probably because I told him not to.

He did send a gorgeous bouquet of flowers but didn't sign them with anything other than his name.

Part of me wants him to show up at my house, sweep me into his arms, and kiss me, so we can live our happily ever after.

The other part of me is glad he's giving me the time.

I've needed it to try to unravel my thoughts. My goals. My life.

Three days ago, I had an epiphany and figured it all out. The moment that everything had gotten messed up.

I'd wanted to have kids my whole life. I loved babysitting for the neighbors. And I was like the Pied

Piper when kids were around. They were always drawn to me. And I loved it.

It wasn't until my senior year in high school when Trent was pushing to get more serious, when he wanted to name our babies and plan our life, that I freaked out. I knew then that I wanted to go away for a while. College. Something. I wanted to see the world. A world that didn't include him. I think I knew deep down that he was always only going to be my high school boyfriend.

And when he pressured me for bigger commitments, like sex, all I could think about was that there was no way I was going to risk my dreams for a few moments of pleasure with a man who wasn't my true love. Add that to the fact that I thought my mother was just a workhorse to my dad and was stuck in a situation she didn't want to be in, it's no wonder I held on to my dreams so tightly. It killed me when my father didn't support me. But even that hadn't stopped me.

And in that moment, I knew that I wasn't going to allow those old fears to hold me back any longer. I knew exactly what I wanted—to be with Carter. To figure out a life together.

I considered going to his house right away to tell him of my decision, but I decided to wait. To make sure.

The last thing I wanted to do was hurt him again.

So, I took some time. And during that time, I planned it all out. I thought about what it would be like, being married to Carter. Where we might live—preferably Carter's Malibu beach house. Our wedding. Believe it or not, I'm even thinking of asking to build a vacation home on the family farm.

I've thought if I want kids and, if so, how many. And I could see Carter and me with kids—a boy and a girl. I'd even like to get a dog.

And I am pretty sure that I'm going to ask Carter to marry me.

The doorbell rings again.

"That must be them!" Lakelyn yells out and then swings open my front door, revealing my older sisters, Brooke and Raine.

"You're here too?" I ask, thrilled to see them.

We hug. They get introduced to Ashlyn, and then Lakelyn says, "We're holding an intervention."

"What does that mean?"

"It means, you have probably been sitting around for weeks, thinking about Carter Crawford," Ashlyn says. "I'm married to a Crawford, so trust me, I understand the appeal. But things weren't easy for me and Cash either. It's hard to give someone your heart, even when you love them. It's scary, right?"

"It is," I agree.

"So, we've decided that we're taking you on a girls' weekend!"

"We're going to drink. Spa. Eat all sorts of food.

And dessert with every meal!" Lakelyn yells.

"Really?" And I can't help but grin.

My sisters are here. Ashlyn is here. A girls' weekend sounds perfect.

"Yes, really," Brooke says. "You need to pack quick. Our driver is waiting for us."

"Where are we going again?" I ask Ashlyn as we're in my room and she's pulling outfits out of my closet.

"Just up the coast," she says.

Once I'm packed and ready to go, we load up in a black SUV and get driven to a small airport that caters to private planes. The same one Carter uses.

Actually, I think, as we drive out onto the tarmac, the jet that we're heading toward looks a lot like Carter's.

Could he be on it?

My heart starts to race with excitement.

But all I can seem to mutter out is, "Um …"

"To answer your question," Ashlyn says, "yes, we're borrowing Carter's plane. But don't tell him."

I laugh out loud. I know her and Cash's story.

I raise an eyebrow at her. "From what I understand, you've borrowed his plane before."

"You bet I did." She turns to my sisters. "You probably haven't heard my and Cash's love story, but we met at a wedding. Harper and Maddox's wedding, specifically. I knew Carter. We were friends, and Cade was my agent, but I had never met

Cash before. At the wedding, my boyfriend broke up with me. I got drunk. Cash showed up. Called me hot ass in that sexy, deep voice of his, and next thing I knew, we'd hooked up, gone to Vegas, and gotten married."

"You what?" Brooke says.

She's by far the most sensible of all of us kids. Never got into trouble.

"It's true!" Ashlyn gushes. "We decided at the wedding—well, I decided—that it was going to be a no-names night. We made up names for each other. I was Hot Ass, and he was Sexy. Those were the names we used in our wedding vows!" she hoots. "Anyway, we had a sexy-as-hell wedding night, and then I snuck out in the morning. Even though I was already in love with him, I had no clue who he was. And get this," she says, slapping Raine's arm, "he told me he was from Seattle—which was where he had been working but he had just taken a job with Cade as a junior talent agent. And his first job was to babysit me." She laughs some more. "And … and … Cade told him he absolutely under no circumstances was to sleep with me. After we'd already done it so many times."

"Wait!" Brooke says. "You got engaged on that talk show, right? His whole family was there?"

"Yes, we did. I was a bit of a mess when we met. Had some issues from my past that I had to work out."

"And he did that adorable video of you sleeping and said he didn't Vegas love you—that he *loved* you."

"Actually, he said, 'I have a confession to make. I don't just Vegas love this girl. I'm madly, impetuously, stupidly, happily, crazy in love with her.'" She clasps her hands together dreamily. "Aren't love stories so romantic?" But then Ashlyn laughs again. "At least they are once they work out. While we were trying to figure our shit out, it was kind of a nightmare. I didn't know what to do. He seemed too perfect to be true."

"And now?" I ask her.

"He's my love slave and happy about it," she jokes. "Seriously, I adore him. He's my best friend. And I can't imagine sharing my life with anyone but him."

"That's how I feel about AJ," Lakelyn gushes.

"So, where are you going on your honeymoon?" I ask. "Now that he's drafted and all."

"He still won't tell me. But I know he's been planning."

"And you know that Carter is helping him," Ashlyn says. "Carter has this town wired, I swear."

"Seems like you do too," I say to Ashlyn.

"Maybe," she says. "Time for a round of shots!"

IT'S A QUICK flight, and to my surprise and slight horror, we pull up to a golf resort and hotel in Half

Moon Bay. The site of our fake engagement.

Does no one see the irony in this?

But then I realize that I never actually told them the name of the hotel. Only that it was a golf resort overlooking the ocean. It's just a coincidence. It has to be.

Either way, we get taken up to a lovely suite with a balcony, where we are served mimosas and given our spa appointments for the day.

I HAVE HAD a full-body scrub, mud treatment, and massage, and I'm lying by the spa pool, feeling quite relaxed. It's not the beach with Carter, but the fact that my sisters flew out here to spend time with me does nothing but confirm my decision.

Taking Carter home with me, even though it was clearly in desperation, was the best thing I ever did. I've talked to my mom twice since I left, and she's been encouraging me on my journey of what she calls my *rediscovery*. My father, who always seems to butt in during some point in our conversation, just asks if I'm back with Carter yet. Of course, he used to want me with Trent, so I've been taking that with a grain of salt.

"All right, ladies," Ashlyn says, glancing at her watch. "We need to head back to the suite. We have hair and makeup coming."

"What for?" I ask her. "I figured we'd just order room service and watch movies or something."

"Are you kidding? We're going out."

"But—" I start to argue.

"We're going downstairs to sit by the outdoor firepit, have cocktails, and then watch the sunset. It's like an event in and of itself. Followed by dinner at the hotel's restaurant. No bachelor party redo," Lakelyn says with a grin.

"Sounds like a plan," I tell them. "The sunsets are amazing here."

I'M READY FIRST, and although I'm chatting away with my sisters and Ashlyn, my thoughts are still on the sunset. Specifically, the sunset I saw at the bridge on the property. How I'm feeling pulled back there in some kind of full-circle moment. The girl who will stand on that bridge now is much different than the one who stood on it a few weeks ago. I want to be struck by the colors and the beauty around me. I want to hear the sounds of the ocean. And I want to feel the warmth of the sun. But I'm not sure that I want to share it with anyone other than maybe Carter.

I consider calling him now. Inviting him to come join me. Now that the draft is over, maybe he could take a few days off. Meet me here after the girls leave.

I take a deep breath and grab my phone. "I need to make a quick call," I say before heading out onto the balcony for a little privacy.

He answers on the first ring. "Hey," he says, his

voice warm and sexy.

"Guess where I am," I tell him.

"On a girls' weekend, I heard," he replies.

"Did Ashlyn tell you where we would be?"

"She mentioned a spa up north."

"I'm at the scene of the crime. The spot of our fake engagement." I let out a chuckle. "Can you believe that?"

"Is that a good thing or a bad thing?" he asks tentatively.

"Good, I think. But that all depends on you."

"On me?"

"Yes. See, I did what I said I would do. I've been thinking, meditating, doing some serious soul-searching, and I know what I want. Not just what I don't want."

"And what do you want, Vale?"

"Well, that's the problem, Carter. I was surprised by this trip. It was a fun surprise, but I had planned to do something more important today. I was going to go to a certain beach in Malibu. I planned to surprise this guy I like by showing up at his house. And I was going to tell him that I love him. And all the things I want in a life with him."

Carter doesn't say anything, but I know he's still on the line because I can hear him breathing.

Finally, he says, "I think the guy would have loved that surprise."

"The girls' trip is just for the weekend, and I can

clear my calendar for the first of the week. What would you say to you coming up here on Sunday and spending some time with me?"

"Well, that all depends," he says, his voice playful now.

"On what?"

"If you promise to show me the bridge. At sunset."

Tears fill my eyes and roll down my freshly done face.

"I can't think of a more perfect place to start a new chapter with you," I tell him.

"Me neither," he says.

I dreamily tell him good-bye and then make my way back inside.

I GET OUT of the hotel robe and grab one of the dresses Ashlyn packed for me. A cute D&G sundress.

She comes into the room and says, "Oh, I think it might be too chilly for that."

"I can just throw a sweater on with it."

"I think this one," she says, pulling out a gorgeous, fit-and-flare, tea-length emerald-green silk-satin dress out of the closet. It features a crew neck and long blouson sleeves set above a banded waist.

"I'm pretty sure that dress wasn't in my closet," I say with a laugh.

She rolls her eyes and grins. "I brought it for you. Actually saw it when AJ and I were shopping and immediately thought of you. It will bring out the green in your eyes."

I give her a hug. "Thank you. Really. For setting all this up. I appreciate it."

She shrugs. "It's nothing. Also, I want you to know, whatever you decide about Carter, we'll stay friends, okay?"

I give her a grin. "Okay."

"No pressure, but when the heck *are* you going to decide?"

"I was planning on going to his house and telling him today, but I ended up here."

"Oh!" she says, looking really surprised. "Uh, well, shoot. We messed up your plans. I'm sorry."

"No need. He was who I called earlier. I told him that I want us to be together. And I invited him to come up here and meet me on Sunday. It's really quite the coincidence that we are here because this is where our fake engagement was supposed to have taken place."

"Well, that's kind of crazy. But good maybe? Like cleansing?"

"Yeah," I say. "It is."

ONCE EVERYONE IS dressed, we go outside to have a drink before sunset.

"Let's go for a walk," Lakelyn says. "The makeup artist was telling me that there's a cool path that goes around the property, and you can get even closer to the ocean and look right over the cliff's edge."

I want to disagree, but it's a miles-long walking path, and we're all wearing high heels. I know my sisters. They'll be ready to sit back down before we make it ten feet. I shouldn't have to worry about us making it all the way to the bridge.

"That sounds amazing!" Brooke says. "I can't wait to explore this place."

We take our drinks and make our way to the path. Where we find two golf carts with drivers, waiting for us.

"Ladies," one says.

"What's this?" I ask.

"Raine mentioned after she had kids that she sort of stopped wearing high heels very often. I didn't want her feet to hurt," Ashlyn says. "So, I called down and asked the valets to give us a lift."

"Perfect," Brooke says.

"But the sun is close to setting," I argue. "I don't want to miss it."

"Oh, don't worry. We won't," the driver says. "We are taking you somewhere it will be even more spectacular."

I let out a sigh and hop in the cart as the bagpipe player who commemorates the sunset starts playing.

We're cruising past the hotel and up a hill when Lakelyn goes, "Hey, look at all the rose petals."

"Oh crap," the driver says. "Why don't you ladies walk around a little, and then we'll take you back?

I'm sure the event planners put them here for wedding photos. I don't want to disturb them with the cart."

And what he says makes sense. So, we get out.

"Look, they lead to a bridge. Come look at this!" Ashlyn says.

And I'm thinking, *No, I'm not going down that path.* It eventually leads to the bridge. And I'm not going there. Not yet. Not without Carter. And certainly not on a bridge filled with flowers waiting for another couple.

But Lakelyn loops her arm around my elbow and leads me down the petal-filled path and around the bend, where I have to blink my eyes, trying to figure out if what I'm seeing is really there.

It's my family.

"What are you doing here?" I can hardly breathe.

My parents, my grandmother and Aunt Helen, my sisters' husbands, and my brother.

My dad walks up to me, gives me a hug, and says, "We decided to take you up on your offer. Come out to see where you live."

"But I don't live here," I say with a laugh as I hug everyone else. "I live in Southern California."

"We might be here for another reason, honey," my mother says. "Why don't you follow the petals and see where they lead you?"

I start to shake.

And tears fill my eyes.

CHAPTER TWENTY-SEVEN
A NEW CHAPTER.

Vale

I FOLLOW THE path, walking on a carpet of rose petals. There are tears in my eyes. I wipe them away since I don't want them blurring my vision. I don't want to miss a moment of this.

There it is. My bridge. Well, not really my bridge, but it's the bridge I had in mind when I described my fake engagement. Surrounded by trees, sitting just beyond a small waterfall.

The sun is about to set, and the landscape is cast in a golden glow.

Lanterns are floating on the water.

A string quartet is softly playing.

But it's not the view that leaves me breathless.

It's the man standing at the center of the bridge, waiting for me.

He looks so handsome in a navy-blue suit, crisp white shirt, and a deep green-and-navy tie knotted at his neck. And I realize his tie matches my dress.

Gotta love family.

Actually, I love him.

"Carter," I say breathlessly as he takes my hands in his.

He gives me a smirk. "I can't think of a more perfect place to start a new chapter with you."

"Stealing my lines now, are you?" I say with a smile. "In that case, I'll take yours and say, me neither."

"Did I get it right?" he asks, sweeping his arm in front of us.

"Actually, it's prettier than I imagined."

"I'm off to a good start," he says.

I notice movement on his side of the bridge and see that his family has taken their place at the base.

I turn around and see mine on the other.

"I can't believe it." My heart is so full that I can barely breathe or think or speak.

He's here. He did all of this.

For me.

PURE MAGIC.

"YOU SHOULD KNOW when we stopped in Iowa to pick your sister up for the draft, I formally asked your father for your hand in marriage. And when I planned all this, I had no idea of what your decision would be or if you'd even made one yet. Either way, I had to give it a shot. I love you, Vale. And I want to spend the rest of my life with you. Here, in California, or even on the farm. I don't care. I just want you."

Her tears sparkle in the light of the setting sun, and the flickering candles in the water make shadows dance on her face. Her hair is aglow, and her dress seems to practically meld into the background. It's like I'm in a fantasy land, the kind of place you would expect to see fairies and unicorns. I can see why she described this moment the way she did because it is magical.

I drop down on one knee, take her hand in mine, and look deep into her eyes. "Will you marry me?"

She leans down, throws her arms around me in a hug, and cries. She's nodding her head against my chest, but she hasn't said anything.

I stand up, picking her up with me.

"Is that a yes?" I murmur in between kisses.

"That's a *hell yes*," she says, grinning at me.

"Shall we seal the deal with something more than a kiss?" I ask her.

"I don't think my father would approve of that," she says in a sultry voice.

"I was thinking of something a little more traditional. And appropriate."

I set her down, reach in my pocket, pull out the ring—her ring—and place it on her finger.

It must translate as a sign of success because I hear an ear-piercing whoop from Blake and cheers from both sides of the bridge.

"Kiss her again!" Grandma shouts.

This causes Vale to laugh through her tears.

"I agree with Grandma. You'd better kiss me again."

So, I do.

AFTER THE PROPOSAL, we go to a private dining room overlooking the ocean and celebrate with our families. It's then that the discussion of wedding planning comes up.

"I was thinking at our farm in Iowa," Mrs. Martin says.

"And I was thinking a Southern California beach wedding," my mom counters.

"We've just gotten engaged," I tell them both, wanting to stop this nonsense before it even gets started.

I want Vale to plan the wedding of her dreams, not have to juggle what our mothers—who have both had weddings of their own already—want.

"That's true," Vale says, grinning at me. "But I know exactly what I want."

"You do?" I ask, not able to hide the shock on my face.

"Yes, I've basically planned our life out in my head. And believe it or not, Carter Crawford, had the girls not come and whisked me off here, I was going to ask you to marry me today."

"Really?" I say, feeling suddenly choked up.

"Really," she says, giving me a kiss. "Provided I didn't walk in and find you kissing some other girl anyway."

Which causes me to laugh along with her.

None of that matters anymore. It's all water under the bridge we just got engaged on.

"So, where will it be—the wedding?" my sister, Chloe, asks.

I look at Vale next to me, wondering if while planning out our life in her head, she planned the wedding out too.

"Well?" I ask, taking her hand into mine.

"California." She smiles. "I was thinking in Napa, on a farm. Seems fitting, doesn't it?"

She looks at me and then glances around the table at our family, who are all teary-eyed at the sentimental suggestion.

"It sounds perfect," I tell her.

"Well, cheers to a future Napa wedding and to a real engagement this time," Chloe says.

"I don't know. I kind of liked being your fake fiancé," I whisper in her ear.

She grins, planting a kiss on my lips as the glasses clink around us. "I think being my real one will have a few more benefits."

ABOUT THE AUTHOR

Jillian Dodd® is a USA Today and Amazon Top 10 best-selling author. She writes fun binge-able romance series with characters her readers fall in love with—from the boy next door in the That Boy series to the daughter of a famous actress in The Keatyn Chronicles® to a spy who might save the world in the Spy Girl® series. Her newest series include London Prep, a prep school series about a drama filled three-week exchange, and the Sex in the City-ish chick lit series, Kitty Valentine.

Jillian is married to her college sweetheart, adores writing big fat happily ever afters, wears a lot of pink, buys way too many shoes, loves to travel, and is distracted by anything covered in glitter.

Made in the USA
Middletown, DE
07 June 2021